Praise for AC Benus
and the *Secret Melville Series*

The sea has got to Redburn, and good. In that one voyage he's ex-
perienced more life in every extreme way than in all his previous years
combined. It's got him hooked like a narcotic, but I feel his good nature
will serve him well and prevent him from falling into the chasm of
hatred and anger that consumed Jackson.
— Stephen *(Redburn)*

The unveiling in this *Typee* gives the reader an extra dimension that
readers in Victorian times might have missed (or could very well have
understood). Great script, AC!
— J.HunterDunn *(Typee)*

After a conflict between Jarl and An'natu, Redburn comforts Jarl, who
breaks down. Their discussion about the bigotry of society is as valid
now as it was in Melville's days. It ends with these beautiful words
spoken by Redburn:

> *" Into the love of equals, we are bound –*
> *You and I are just alike –*
> *One to the other, unbroken."*

Thanks, AC. Another great script.
— J.HunterDunn *(Omoo)*

You've captured the spirit of Victorian novels quite well – not a jot of
happiness anywhere, and conventional morality reigns supreme.
Where may we expect to see the workhouse, or the beadle, or grimy
smokestack belching out noisome vapors to settle over brick tenement
terraces?

More please, and pass the opium so I can have a pleasant dream.
— ColumbusGuy *(Pierre)*

I like symmetry in architecture; music. It has an aesthetic appealing
quality. And I find it in *Pierre* as well. Redburn, Emily and Sara make
one side of the building, while Pierre, Lucy and Isabelle form the other,
completing the symmetrical structure of the whole script.
— J.HunterDunn *(Pierre)*

Praise for AC Benus and
"Becoming Real"

This is a jewel of a short story. There's a type of personal detail given to each of the people in it that makes me think of Somerset Maugham. I love beautiful prose too, and this is written so well that it's a joy to read.

The apple tree sees it all, doesn't it? . . . as it slowly falls apart. But it will bloom again in the spring, and that's the good part.
—Stephen *(In the Cards)*

What a way to start the journey! I really like how Josh experiences it. As the other reviews before me have pointed out, it's hard to walk away from this chapter without feeling at least one piece of it. Everything this chapter brings up and puts out there is something we can all go and see in reality. That makes the impact even heavier. That night could've gone horribly wrong for Josh in so many ways. Thank goodness it was a good guy who picked him up and showed him around. Very interested to see what the next short story brings.
—Twisted Dreemz *(The Meeting in the Park)*

I don't think it's fair for you to tell my story so well. However, mine wasn't set in a big city, and it was a bipolar guy who helped me cope. Otherwise, the emotions are identical. Bravo!!!!
—Cole Matthews *(The Meeting in the Park)*

I am quite fascinated by the power dynamic between younger and older Gay men. Younger queer people generally have a detestable inexperience about them, but their youth is always envied. Older men can use their money and authority to pull rank over younger Gay men, but ultimately, their wisdom is respected. The exchange between Josh and Dick was quite fascinating. I have dated older men and I can totally relate to the events of this chapter. There is a sadness, sometimes, associated with the navigation of the LGBTQ+ world. I hope Josh does not let this deter him or scare him from his journey of finding himself.
—Bryce Lee *(The Old Man)*

This is so good, so relatable to me it hurts. I am literally cringing as pains pierce my guts reading this. Maybe it's because we are roughly from the same time or maybe our experiences were similar. Regardless, it is so fantastic you have me wincing every paragraph. Brutal and real.
— Cole Matthews *(The Old Man)*

Also Available from AC Benus

Mojo, a Sex Comedy and Satire
A modern reimagining of Petronius' ancient novel Satyricon *set in Trump's America of conmen, the conned, the ultra-rich, the sexy and the downright silly. "A laugh riot!"*
ebook: ISBN 9781734561074; paperback: ISBN 9781734561050

One Hundred and Fifty-Five Sonnets for Tony
A bold testament to love
ebook: ISBN 9781953389114; paperback: ISBN 9781953389107; hardback: ISBN 9781953389121

Becoming Real: One Coming Out in Seven Short Stories
Setting, St. Louis. Time, 1990 – a young man overcomes the odds
ebook: ISBN 9781953389305; paperback: ISBN 9781953389282; hardback: ISBN 9781953389299

Carême in Brighton, a Culinary Murder Mystery
Mayhem, intrigue and good food at the Prince Regent's seaside villa
ebook: ISBN 9781953389213; paperback: ISBN 9781953389176; hardback: ISBN 9781953389206

Walks With Leporello, an Airedale Remembered
An exploration of Love, God and Dog
ebook: ISBN 9781953389268; paperback: ISBN 9781953389251; hardback: ISBN 9781953389275

Also Available from AC Benus

The Secret Melville Series
Seven filmscripts based on the sea novels of Herman Melville
Follow our eponymous hero, from age 19 and his first taste of the sea, until he's one of America's most promising writers in New York City and its surrounding countryside.

Volume 1. Secret Melville:
Redburn & Typee
ebook: ISBN 9781953389022
paperback: ISBN 9781953389039

Volume 2. Secret Melville:
Omoo & Mardi & Moby-Dick
ebook: ISBN 9781953389046
paperback: ISBN 9781953389053

Volume 3. Secret Melville:
White-Jacket & Perrie and the Ambiguities
ebook: ISBN 9781953389060
paperback: ISBN 9781953389077

Same Love *(Contributor)*
Short Story Anthology: a compendium offered during the time of the COVID pandemic, D.K. Daniels, Editor

---

Poetry Available from AC Benus

Hymenaios, or The Marriage of the God of Marriage
A Classical style myth in 2,600 lines of Blank Verse
ebook: ISBN 9781953389091; paperback: ISBN 9781953389084

Summer 2020 – Hell in a Handbasket
A contender for the Pulitzer Prize in poetry, 2021, this collection grapples with the year of pandemic, racial injustice and environmental crisis
ebook: ISBN 9781953389015; paperback: ISBN 9781953389008

The Thousandth Regiment
A Translation of and Commentary on Hans Ehrenbaum-Degele's First World War Poems "Das tausendste Regiment"
ebook: ISBN 1657220583; paperback: ISBN 9781657220584

A Man in a Room, and other poems
Verse following the year when the poet was 21 years old
ebook: ISBN 97817345103; paperback: ISBN 978173456107

The Easiest Thing in the World, and other poems
Marking the third anniversary of the Pulse Nightclub terror attack
ebook: ISBN 9781734561029; paperback: ISBN 9781734561036

Rima Fragmenta, or Fragments of a Rift
Fifty Sonnet for Kevin
ebook: ISBN 9781734561005; paperback: ISBN 9781734561012

First Love: Poems for Ross
For everyone's first love; both bitter and sweet
ebook: ISBN 9781734561081; paperback: ISBN 9781734561098

Poetry Available from AC Benus

Demon Dream
Redemption and shared humanity shine in this retelling of a medieval Japanese legend
ebook: ISBN 9781953389138; paperback: ISBN 9781953389145

Audre Lorde Knows What I Mean – 2021 in Review
A follow-up to Summer 2020, *this collection grapples with the year of the Gop-led Capitol insurrection, racial injustice and the death throes of the environment*
ebook: ISBN 9781953389015; paperback: ISBN 9781953389008

Mikhail Kraminsky, and other poems
Two collections of early poems exploring the pain of youth and being closeted
ebook: ISBN 9781953389152; paperback: ISBN 9781953389169

One Hundred and Fifty-Five Sonnets for Tony
A bold testament to love
ebook: ISBN 9781953389114; paperback: ISBN 9781953389107; hardback: ISBN 9781953389121

Love Looked at Me and Laughed – Poems for Brian
Love is not always easy. Poems to/for/about my first boyfriend
ebook: ISBN 9781953389237; paperback: ISBN 9781953389220
hardback: ISBN 978-1-953389-24-4

Love is Love (Contributor)
Poetry Anthology: In aid of Orlando's Pulse victims and survivors, Lily G. Blunt, Editor, 2016
ebook: ISBN 153514369X; paperback: ISBN 153514369X

AC Benus

an AC Benus Impression
San Francisco

Grateful acknowledgement is here offered
for the support and encouragement
I've received on the literary site
www.gayauthors.org.

ISBN 978-1-953389-34-3 (ebook)
ISBN 978-1-953389-33-6 (paperback)

Cover photo:
Miguel á Padriñán / pexels.com

Heart vignette:
Freepik.com

Library of Congress Control Number: 2023902940

Poem No. 1
A Sendoff for Sunny

Sonnet:

The way your hands would find my head to you
And want it as though never satisfied,
Thereby slaying what apprehensions do,
While caresses caught on my every side . . .
Yet age will snatch gone what you praised of me;
The moments take each part their due to them;
And the years creep on my discrepancy,
Grafting age onto what your praise did stem.
But if in nature's plan, mistakes are made,
And this is but one of them, I have scope
To see sterility will not be laid
At Love's feet who always finds child in hope.
      Yet I will still recall those hands of yours,
      Knowing where human glory keeps its stores.

Poem:

The first full yellow of Spring
has given itself to green
while blossoms surrender youth
for fruitful transformations
of the summer yet to be.

These with each other we saw
and counted them as they fell;
too soon to fall away ourselves
they watched you go from my side
while telling me what could be.

Now they all wait for the one
that will not in this world bear
a useful fruit of issue
but still better than the rest,
for every heart comes alive
for the length of time it lives.

I have squares to mark the days
and lines to tell me the hour;
until the day you come back
they will see my company
and beside me long for you.

I have the colors you lack
to witness what you've not seen
but they much too soon will fade
from wayward to a purpose
and create themselves anew.

What the markers cannot do
is see more than this struggle;
they can't give me what I want
any more than bright gives dull
a rising vent to sunshine.

Can you love me well enough
to thus rouse a Spring in me;
big enough to flood you back;
sweet to the point of ever
being what you want of me?

Unlovely I may yet seem
but your love might be a sun
to hurry me to myself;
it holds me to pencil point
with leaves needing you to grow.

About me eyes are opening,
giving themselves to a life,
in eager hope of knowing
the light from which sprang their change
from darkness to certainty.

But can I love you enough
to there rouse a Spring in you;
big enough to flood me back;
sweet to the point of ever
being what I want of you?

Sonnet:

If I too easily ask for your love,
And you upon no grounds can confer it,
Then gone's the promise of that vouchsafed love
By my lassitude and will to show it.
Though Spring by each drop of rain increases,
Scarcely can its value be seen in here,
Where this rendered fold of want re-creases
Old forms to fit new desires most dear.
But I want your arms to round me descend
And hold me like none the other mattered,
Where yet together we the Spring can spend
If love between us the ice has shattered.
 For the next time I have you to hold me,
 You'll be surprised how well held back you'll be!

Poem No. 2

Adrift with sleep between your arms
    I dream of that love to wear like pride,
floating beneath your countenance strong,
    between your arms and evening's side.

Some wear their love like a passion
    and too soon find it all worn away,
then in its loss, make an obsession
    that the morning never finds the day.

Fools feel it something to command,
    to deem order to blind confusion,
then grow to shaking their vacant hand,
    pleading for its shameful retention.

But I twix your arm and dark night,
    made drowsy by your firm correction,
can see myself in your loving sight,
    adrift your love's sweet conviction.

Poem No. 3

Sonnet:

What monument to erect in your face
That might outlive my wont of deserving;
To find in a ream of paper the space
To take this mute want beyond lip-serving.
Love me like Death will love me tomorrow,
Like that act of living could deliver
My soul from your hands into her sorrow,
Boxlike to be her eternal lover.
But who in my hereafter may I move
To make this day alive in every eye
Which might borrow my view of you to prove
That yearning fresh can find form more than sigh.
    I love you, Sunny, and will not
        live an afterlife of shame
    For never having writ the word
        next to your belovèd name.

Poem No. 4

What dictionary could tell it to you,
like all the words therein kept,
could sigh what you gave me
in the days we have just left.

So put Mister Webster away,
his legacy won't breathe account,
with passion or fire sufficient,
to spirit how much you are loved.

If I were born without a soul,
and could not live long to devise me one,
then I'll count the days and love I've got
enough to have lived . . .

    if not forever . . .

    at least a day enough.

<u>A Thank You for Sunny</u>

Poem No. 5

With boneless fingers, reach they yet beyond the grave
　　for that undecayed passion, never reached by what they say,
　　but whose smolder still lingers, grasping ever from night to day –
　　sweet stanching compassion, take me, as yet in death they lay.

Though all-conquered were, the flesh of their belovèds,
　　the same motives to them then, to longing Night's encover,
　　where cotton or linen stir, but where contentment might hover,
　　moves the throb of my pen, and makes me of it its lover.

How can they yet live, though melted away are they;
　　what once beat them out a life, long past those summer days seen,
　　for they words this longing give, as Beauty consumed them not clean,
　　leaving thoughts to suffice, as the fuel for Ages between.

In the wont of it, shall I live to discover,
　　and I know it very true, but accept Death sneaks on me,
　　though alive I am and fit, always looking for it to see –
　　content to burn me through, that pyre will be the life of me.

Poem No. 6

How shall I live this love to prove
when by these tepid degrees,
some passionless toddler's move,
one word to another but falls to these.
How shall I live my love in fact
when by timid themes I try
an inspired task, with insipid act,
as my vigor-less tune can only sigh.
How shall I live this love to prove.

Poem No. 7

Sonnet:

Crouching, creeping, old; rubbing plans together they
Brim with toothless mouths and screeching most odious.
They pass round hate from one till it torrents convey
And but whets benediction with blood-red malice.
Too cruel are you, how like to they can be
When one moment takes your blessing away
And the wide world forgets its memory
Of how little life we have used today.
Yet for the hags, one eye goes round from which they spy
All the horror they could only scheme to thus make,
And envy your only too invidious eye
Watching the love-hacking furor your spirits take.
 But their hate is just their job
  and Fateful benefice 'tis,
 When likened to the careless hate
  your anger is.

Poem No. 8

Lost in thoughts of your caress
    The afternoon creeps away
Seconds, the hours seem less
    Till the evening hours cleanse the day
Of its purposeful nonsense
    And I can find myself again
Lost in your caress.

Poem No. 9

Sonnet:

And so, how could I love you any more?
If all the stars did join in for effect,
How could they add to my affections' score . . . ?
This some lovers say to their loves direct.
From up ahead I see, from stile to stile goes,
She through the lonely world moving content
To watch one hand caress the head it knows,
But glides near to hear how much of it's meant.
So I dull upon the floor wonder which,
The sun in my eye or the moon in sight,
Gives me the best estimable comfort rich –
A cold-glowing rock or my love burning bright.
    But each evening finds me not as before;
    She finds I've found I love you all the more.

Poem:

Whisper words of love to me
That I know I am alive
Hold the hand of me
That I might the night survive.

For how shall the morning
Makes amends if not so
I discover a deeper something growing
From the love you swear I know.

Whisper words of death to me
Of how they conquer all they know
And how by your love I'll see
For us, it will not be so.

Poem No. 10

単語かいしたで,
まわがい いつしょうに,
のずむはなしたいが,
愛していますそ。

    In borrowed words,
    Mistakes included,
    What I want to say is
    I love you so.

Poem No. 11

When your eyes cast out at me,
I sometimes wish through them I could see.

Poem No. 12

Prelude:

As I labor on this freak of love,
in green and yellow
and North African blue
torture tables
wearing tortuous ties
all my work was in
but the service of vain
that found but smiles
and succumb to my pain
but I self-pity
forms a child half-conceived
to make a better humor
out of my affairs
simply by adding

Czech hanging glass
off of all my ideas
making black and blue
the work I offered
while Czech glass
hangs off all my love.

    Poem:

But like a flower in the bud,
Your opportunities wait for me
Where spring is ever just in seed,
When your embraces rain down on me.

Though work and change swings and burns
From contempt to love, to love of hate,
The dial of my love never turns
That it doesn't tell the position of my fate.

Like want itself, I think of you,
At that last kiss you gave,
And I long such lengths for you
That never I'll be the same

Like a flower in the bud
My day of returns awaits
When no other sun instead
Will hold my time as waste.

Postlude:

Red cut glass
player pianos
black like wood
furniture dropping out
that plopping down
marble pretense
pushing wood's intent
of an honest life
all that might
make their aim
the intent of my despair
but I have knowledge
like a secret in me burning
that I can pass without a care
all that goes with a silly age,
to the future give my longing
when to your arms I will care
to have no other knowledge
than the touch of your love burning.

Poem No. 13

Love's answer from *The Passionate Pilgrim* No. 20:
  The Passionate Shepherd to His Belovèd Boy Alexis

Live with me and be my love,
And we will all the pleasures prove
That hills and valleys, dales and fields,
And all the craggy mountain yields.

There will we sit upon the rocks,
And see the shepherds feed their flocks,
By shallow rivers, by whose falls
Melodious birds sing madrigals.

There will I make thee a bed of roses,
With a thousand fragrant posies,
A cap of flowers, and a kirtle
Embroidered all with leaves of myrtle.

A belt of straw with ivy buds,
With coral clasps and amber studs;
And if these pleasures may thee move,
Then live with me, and be my love.
                        —Christopher Marlowe

  Sunny,

        With these borrowed words have I tried
        To grab and bring you by my side.
        Tonight the beginning might begin
        If these and I your heart can win.

Poem No. 14

Sonnet:

Reach deep in me and take my heart in hand –
Slip around me as in our nascent form
When mere membrane and bone couldn't demand
Us to be two beats apart like the norm.
If through the wilds of my rug tonight,
You find me by soothing troubles away,
Watch what you've retrieved in me spread delight
As in an ear, breath-like, the L-word say.
Touch the husk knowing full well what I am –
Only matter in decay whose green is gone,
But desire moves as only virgin springs dam,
That near you might run barefoot through the dawn.
    Say you love me more than timely
        form could ever likely do;
    Say forever's but a sapling
        when pared to the love of you.

Poem No. 15

Haiku Stanza:

In the blackest bowl
Sits the orangest kinmokusei,
Fragrancing our love.

Poem No. 16
An Apology

Sonnet:

If I were a real poet, I'd tilt the skies
with me as I set motion to this act,
writing boldly black the breadth and size
of my times seemingly, but of me in fact.
Yet, what am I but a manly Harpy,
screeching through one love, ripping another;
the feeding madness feigning therapy,
with no peace for me, comfort for the other.
In my dreams I used to fly, I can swear,
but such an ideal has fallen in kind
and smolders hatefully before me there
when I see your eyes watching from behind.
    And yet, just say you love me like before,
    And on that breeze, watch man and poet soar.

Poem:

She said, "Do you think love is forever . . . ?"
I thought that's a question to tell my age;
if yes, a boy it proves me; if no,
how much have I paid to become a man.

"If two people are in love," she said then,
"the one who plays the deeper role in love
will always be the loser; strength's not enough
to keep what words alone used to hold."

She asked me whether I was man or boy;
if my sky were cast with anxious gloom.
I told her, "As long as youth will be young,
and I getting old, so love urbane will be eternal."
This I believe, this I say to you.

Sonnet:

The more I try to make us one, the more
My heavy-handed mixtures fails to work,
But makes a mire to estrange our score
While touch cuts, and wider the rifts assert.
The kinmokusei have fallen from the tree
And backwardly like stars to the dark earth
Through the air sightlessly now tumble free –
Liberty from the branch; prisoner by birth.
But take my hand and hold it near your heart,
Don't push me out of you to careless night;
Make me substantial from this tainted start
So that a phoenix from the mud takes flight.
    Say you love me, for I know it's yet so;
    Let the truth rise, and all its glory show.

Poem No. 17

Time fly on silky silence
till my sorrow of today
be folded in your arms tomorrow
and there we'll a portrait paint
of a love so true that gold
blushes aluminum cheap before it

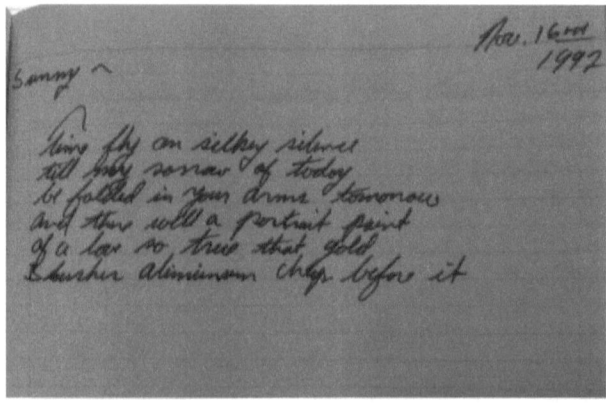

Poem No. 18
A Tardy Little Valentine for Sunny

Sonnet:

In the still time of the coming morning
The gray sky reflects your still sleeping face
And I wonder what token love-shorning
Could fair this day enough to match that grace.
A bushel of camellias, strongly red;
Or a bunch of plum blossoms plucked for you;
Or some shy Adonis poking his head
Blondly away from lovesick Love's kissing due.
But could bold color or my dull fustian
Hold as my hands can in untroubled clime,
Waiting for day to break the frustration
And guide the world to love a better time?
    For then I'll see the narcissic daffodils turn
    To envy your soul, and there, true beauty learn.

Poem No. 19

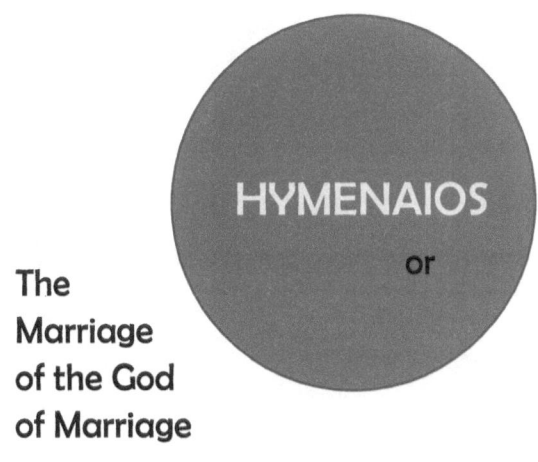

HYMENAIOS

or

The
Marriage
of the God
of Marriage

Prelude

Sonnet:

Outside, winter plays one last trick on spring,
As through the room of your brain, a fever
Makes your perspiring head its plaything,
While I hold you to play heat's deceiver.
How to say I love you if not like this –
No knife box could sharpen my demeanor
More than pressing lips on your brow to kiss,
And pull back with intent all the keener.
So rest, and when morning finds you again,
It will see me still holding on, and true –
The metaphysical reasons found when
The tale I've woven finds its end in you.
    So drift in sleep and open the portal
    To see how love makes us more than mortal.

PART ONE:
THE KEMPT KATHROS

Hymen and Myiscus strolled through the street,
Aglow, calmly with that one sensation
Achieved by what a long afternoon's bath
Instills into a person's wellbeing.
Their minds at peace, they might move through the noise　　5
Without really being a part of it.
Free from the mundane trade and its bustle,
They could enjoy the people on parade.
City Agoras were almost always packed[1]
In the midafternoons, and this one was　　10
No different, as users rushed all about.
On this day, half-old ladies browsed for new
Things to chitchat with other half-old bags.
Their laughs and flying hands sailed on the air
Like so many doves in congregation　　15
Cooing from stall to stall, but buying not.
Sometimes hands would creep from pendulous veils –
The kind only worn by the long-married –
Extending a touch to a bolt of cloth
Vendors might extoll as superior.　　20
Between, in front, and all round the adults,
Spirited little boys moved like sparrows

---

[1] Agora is Greek for town market, or the central plaza of a community.

Snatching booty from slow-witted pigeons.
At waist level, their heads – some dark; some fair –
Played unintelligible games of chance: *25*
Weaving in; weaving out, with back-glances
To spy places they've been for pursuers,
Only to screech delight when they found one.
For then, one would two, three or four become
Scurrying about in chaotic play.   *30*
Also, there were stalls offering flowers,
For this was the main route a worshiper
Would take to get to the Acropolis.
Grapevine and delicate dill were woven
Together as garlands of godly gifts.   *35*
As offerings to those sacred on high,
They hung from cedar poles sellers hefted
Moving among the crowd and crying loud.
Other votives swagged beams of grounded stalls,
Twining myrtle, rosebuds and violets   *40*
Into hefty chains of devotionals.
Pilgrims could match blossom to deity,
Choosing the right flower to help their quest:
The thorned bud to beseech love someone's way;
The pale pansy, a frank apology   *45*
For one's blundering through a transgression.
Likewise to buy, incense, oil and honey
Sweeten might the gods' most desired favor,
For gods like men can most appreciate
Contrition laced with tears and subornment.   *50*
The bright day shone down on the bright two lads,
Smiling at each other in observing
The comings and goings of their own times.
Myiscus was the taller of the two.
His eyes were large and rich, and in one look   *55*
Could take more from people than was offered;
See a bit of what they wanted to hide.
Many told the boy of his dark beauty,
But Myiscus did not see it himself.
He thought Hymenaios the more handsome,   *60*
For daylight loved to play with his friend's hair,

Which was more like itself – an auburn-blond.
So too Hymen's brows and lashes were bright
And sparkled when he blinked out in the day.
Mirrors of his soul they were like, and blue.   *65*
They and the sandy freckles strewing his arms
Bespoke him a true son of Helios;
Beneath his father was he happiest.
Both young men had just turned eighteen years old
And were, and still stayed, each other's best friend,   *70*
First playing the games that little boys do,
Then growing up, into the attentions
Of the men of Athens who would teach them,
And they loving every minute of it.
Myiscus, whose deep-hued and free glances,   *75*
Flashed smiles not weaned upon sweet innocence –
While for Hymen, his face not apple pure –
Moving with the assurance of a god
Caused scowls to meet them from every dog's boy,
And could draw wistful sighs from all the men.   *80*
"Did you see that!" the taller one inquired,
Nudging his buddy to peer through the crowd.
Hymen looked where guided. "No, Myiscus—"
"That rascal boy took a bite of apple,
'Fore putting it back in that lady's pile."   *85*
Hymen laughed, seeing what his friend had meant.
"Some maid," he mused, "will get surprised at home."
Myiscus watched Hymen's face in profile,
First seeing the gracile lips form a grin
Before cracking a good-natured chuckle.   *90*
"Someone," the redhead said, "should give that kid
A good, old-fashioned round of spanking, huh?"
Myiscus darkly laughed. "Oh, in that case,
"I think I know just the guy who'll do it."
To Hymen's confused pout, he continued,   *95*
"That randy Meleager would be first
To form a line of needed volunteers."
"Well…" The sun-kissed boy laughed, squeezing his friend.
"You'd know about that man's well-used 'cudgel,'
Having many times been servant to it."   *100*

29

For that, Myiscus gave his pal a punch,
Though it was pulled and merely aimed squarely
For the top of his companion's shoulder.
Hymen reacted with more laughter and
Drew up his arms, plus a single knee, for 105
Needless defense from his friend's fake fury.
But as the two boys settled to quiet,
And resumed their slow homeward migration,
Hymenaios came to an abrupt stop.
Myiscus, too busy chirping, just moved 110
Along the crowded pathway up ahead.
It took him a moment to see his friend
Was lacking from his side, and looked about.
Hymen stood statue-still, staring into
A market booth of the most usual kind. 115
Though he puzzled what the interest could be,
Myiscus retread his way back among
The ever-squawking flocks of crumb shoppers.
His neck craned to see what had snared his friend's
So-clearly rapped interest at the moment. 120
Rejoined once more, Myiscus thought to speak,
For all he saw was the commotion of
The cooing and clawing of a bright bolt
Of what the merchant said was pure purple
From the far shores of rich, exotic Tyre. 125
Then Hymen slapped his arm, for his friend was
Looking into the completely wrong stall.
Myiscus had his thoughts interrupted,
Witnessing his pal's hand move urgently
Up to the center of Myiscus' chest 130
"She's the loveliest girl I've ever seen…."
Hymen's dreamy tone made Myiscus stare,
But at what, he was still not quite so sure.
He saw a typical flower seller
With a hefty auntie pushing in front. 135
It appeared like an ordinary scene,
And then, as when the curtains of a shrine
Are drawn back to reveal the sacred form,
Her bulk stepped aside, and Myiscus saw

A lovely young woman shopping garlands.   140
Hymen by her appeared transfixed; his eyes
Staring blankly; his hands falling listless
Drooped down to wait uselessly by his sides;
And the young man's grinning faded to naught.
Myiscus returned to the girl causing   145
This stymieing effect upon his friend.
The graceful sweep of the clothing she wore
Came up to rest on her head in white folds
Caressing her great chestnut-colored locks.
He watched her delicate fingers at work   150
Around a wreath, picking one lucky rose
To invite surrender of its sweet scent.
"Myiscus, look. Have you ever seen such –
Seen such a beautiful girl in your life?
If prone I was to swearing, then I'd say   155
She must descend to us from among gods –
Perhaps on a holy errand for them –
For our Agora merchandise is base
When next to the tribute of her beauty."
The smile of Hymenaios then bloomed large   160
As it shone warmly on his companion,
Adding, "Surely she can't be one of us."
Myiscus, for his part, had to swallow
The confusion in his gullet, for this
Turn of sudden affairs was uncalled for.   165
He tried to laugh it off. "Already, friend…?
Is your heart so fickle and quick to change,
For only an hour ago at Gym
You cried *'Oh, Alexis, beautiful boy!*
You're too painful to see but not be near,'"—   170
Myiscus swooned, imitating his chum—
"'Not to rest in your arms all through the night
Is penance more than my life is now worth.
Oh, Alexis; my Alexis!' you said."
Back to the newfound girl, Myiscus looked,   180
Asking softly, "So, Hymen, what has changed…?"
Sunlight playing in his hair, his blue eyes

As welkin as the azure sky, he said,
"But *she's* not like the rooster-boys we love,
Strutting tall, in their god-given beauty,   *185*
Melting all hearts in fear of their confidence.
No, no. This girl is like a star-born pearl,
Who descending from the phoenix tears must
Be caught by human hands to keep her from
Contact with the damning soil of the world.   *190*
Rough-heart boys will always save each other,
Though shallow in life and cruel to the faults
Of all 'cept the ones they can't see in themselves.
But gems like this girl must be admired
And protected from the damning faults of men."   *195*
How astounded was Myiscus, for here
The truth of it was laid bare in his friend's
Sunny, tender but pain-filled countenance.
His truest friend was in love with this girl.
A moment of desolation found him,   *200*
For though he never cared romantically,
To Myiscus, Hymen was his best love;
The one to whom he could say anything
Without dread of scorn or loss of favor.
But now, he could see the end of that.   *205*
The pit of his stomach hurt, but he joked,
"So, she can't be one of us, you think, huh…?"
Hymen, in a flash of youthful deftness,
Moved to stand before his pal with hands
Draped loosely on Myiscus' shoulders.   *210*
"What is it you mean, my friend; you know her?"
After a teasing moment of silence,
Myiscus revealed, "She's my sister's friend."
Hymen's eyebrows evoked his disbelief.
"No, no, it' true," Myiscus asserted.   *215*
"She's the daughter of Stratos, the rich one
Who's the merchant of fine wine to The State.
She and my sister study together…."
Myiscus stopped, for the head of his mate
Lolled on Hymen's arm and appeared quite pained.   *220*
"If you know her," Hymenaios whispered,

32

"Then to me, reveal but a single thing—"
Myiscus nodded, feeling quite concerned.
"Tell you what?" he asked. "Her name," Hymen said.
The darker of the two replied simply: *225*
"It's Kathros, meaning the 'one who is pure.'"
Hymenaios, much moved in love before,
Loosened his hold on his buddy and stood –
Watching again the girl peruse the stall –
To see his love ennobled with a name.   *230*
"My sweet, perfect Kathros – I should have known
What the gods designed to have you be called."
Myiscus cleared his throat, shaking his pal.
"But dear Hymen, you better *know* right now
This girl's father is so strict, she's never   *235*
Allowed to see us men. The only time
She's permitted to go out in public
Is on her usual Thursday votive.
So today it must be she'll buy a wreath
And offer it to Artemis – you know –   *240*
Praying for a rich husband like daddy."
He winked and gave Hymen a little nudge.
But when the boy didn't respond in kind,
Myiscus thought he'd quickly add, "Her maid,
The selfsame one we spy before us here,   *245*
Never leaves her alone for a second,
Be it any time of the day or night."
This crushing blow he'd whispered in his ear
Knowing it'd hurt, but the truth always does.
For his part, Hymen watched the maid and girl   *250*
For whom he had so suddenly fallen
Pay for a wreath of pink poppies enlaced
As strands about tied-boughs of evergreen.
The shrewd lad manning the flower business –
No doubt filling in for some gone adult –   *255*
Even dared to bite the coin that fed him.
Satisfied, he bowed out of their way and
Allowed the two women to leave the stall.
Hymen and Myiscus watched them ascend
The crowded streets, heading for the temples.   *260*

33

"Near her, I simply wish to be a while;
With her, I merely want to speak awhile…."
Myiscus again saw his friend's features
Be overwrought to the point of sorrow.
Then his auburn chum said with quick shrugging,   265
"I'm not sure what's happened to me either,
But what is there I can do about it?
For I only wish to be by her side.
Myiscus, help me. I'm serious, I'm….
"I am truly in love, love beyond bounds."   270
Hymen, whom he loved, was begging for help,
But Myiscus had no ready ideas.
He thus sputtered, "It's getting a bit late.
I should go home so they don't start to fret."
With that, he tried to go, but Hymen's look   275
Made him hesitate a moment longer.
Though he wished to soothe the sadness away,
He found he lacked the knowledge to do it.
Myiscus succumbed to the come time when
An awkward boy wants to comfort his friend,   280
And wash mis'ry from the face before him,
But merely stands there as the moment goes.
Turning then, he walked, watching the cobbles
Pass beneath his feet as he headed home.
All of a sudden, he recalled something,   285
Rotating to walk backwards a few steps,
Calling out, "We're still on for tonight, right?"
Hymen, awoken from his reverie,
Hastened to assure his friend. "Yes, of course.
I'll be at your house by the strike of eight."   290
His tone changed, yelling: "Watch where you're going!"
But it was too late. He saw Myiscus
Stumble backwards over a vendor's crate.
Hymen laughed as the angry peddler then
Began to chase his klutzish companion.   295
Once the commotion found its conclusion,
Hymen's passing glance lingered on the stall
Where he'd first discovered his sweet Kathros.
Going in, he bought the garland and rose –

Though still tight within its protective bud – 300
His beloved girl had sanctioned with a kiss.
Then straight home he went, and into the court.
There he bent down before his household shrine.
Below its miniature pediment,
Two Corinthian columns glowed red paint. 305
Between these were a pair of paneled doors
Resembling an ordinary cupboard's.
Hymen lit an amber chunk of incense,
And its strongly divine fumes filled the house.
With reverential hands, he then began 310
The opening of the doors, and revealed
The wooden statue of Aphrodite,
Her flesh gracefully hued in ivory.
Behind the love goddess, on the shrine's walls,
Blue skies were alive with white doves in flight, 315
Their beaks holding ribbons and gauzy clothes
For their demure mistress to array her
Once she'd stepped from her private bath – the sea.
Hymen untied the swag and strung it there,
Secured by the columns on either end. 320
Kneeling, he saw something unprepared for.
The rose of Kathros had opened and bloomed.
The boy clasped his hands and quietly prayed:

> "*Assist me, Goddess, when I woo her heart to me;*
> *Show her a greater love than mine, she'll never see.*" 325

PART TWO:
A BORROWED FLOWER STALL

Same day a week later, Hymen waited,
Amid bustling crowds, for his time to come.
But Chronos himself had begun to slow –
At least to the bright boy whose clock started
Only the moment he first laid eyes on   *5*
The purest of the pure, his kempt Kathros.
With him, on this sunny market Thursday,
He'd brought a sole ambition in his heart.
So now he stood impatiently shifting
One restless foot beneath him at a time,   *10*
His vigilant gaze scouring down the hill
As temple-goers made their way up it.
Inside his head, true love's nature beckoned
That he upon it ruminate, and know
Although a week already, the sudden   *15*
Birth of it in Hymen's core was like fire;
He'd seen her, and struck by Eros, melted.
'Are things more noble just the same?' he mused,
But as so often is the case, not one
Godly answer gave up explanation.   *20*
He stood to attention, spotting the maid
A few hundred feet down the shopping street,
And then a second more, there was Kathros.
Hymen put his right-brained scenario

37

Into its most immediate deploy –
The timing could not have been more perfect,
As the same lad as last week was in charge.
Hymen dashed through the street, into the stall.
The boy, who was perhaps twelve or thirteen,
Pulled himself like a magnet to the gold
Hymen held up to the youth's eyelevel.
Once drawn in like a catch within a net,
A reassuring hand Hymenaios
Placed upon the young entrepreneur's neck.
Gently massaging for reassurance,
Hymen bent to whisper in the boy's ear:
"Lend me your stall, young man, that I might work
For a mere ten minutes' economy.
You will get the better in the exchange."
So said, the gold slipped into the open
Clutches of the mercenary young man.
After the coin was bit and tested true,
The lad skipped out in another moment,
Making Hymen the shop's proprietor.
He walked behind the wreaths and garlands,
And soon the maid came clomping by, clearing
A pathway like the prow of a warship,
In whose wake safely drifted the maiden.
After they had neared, and the nurse gone by –
Gaudy and worldly things distracting her
From up ahead on the loud thoroughfare –
Hymen held out a fine wreath of cypress,
Embroidered all between its lacy fronds
With the palest of wisteria sprigs.
He held it for Kathros, and her alone.
Slowly, the girl by scanning other blooms
Must have found them to be overwhelming,
For the evergreen and soft lilac sprays
Planted a fresh plot in her perspective.
The young man hoped he could lure her closer,
And thought of the irony of the boy
Quick tempted with matters material;

Only with the girl he knew that not coin
But the substance of his spirit drew her
Like a sunflower seed to open blue sky.   *65*
His ploy was effective, for Kathros stopped.
Holding the arrangement herself, she asked
Its origin, its quality and price.
Hymen replied, "Wrought by hands too-earthly,
Nonetheless fit tribute for the divine;   *70*
It's worth is yet untested, but its price
Will prove to the tooth its true purity."
Thus listening, a new cast came to her,
Her eyes seeming to understand his words,
Although her conscious mind could not grasp them.   *75*
In boldness then, he dared to touch her hand,
Seeing within her stare, the jolt both felt.
"Take it, dear lady," Hymenaios said.
"For any goddess that might receive it —
This wreath – from your blessèd fingers, will know   *80*
Divine virtue can live in us as well."
Regrouping herself and looking for Nurse,
But seeing the woman nowhere nearby,
Kathros took the cypress and wisteria,
Imparting a shy smile for the beauty   *85*
Of the flower boy giving it her thus.
When she turned and sailed back towards her maid,
Hymen's heartbeat throbbed close upon his throat,
Feeling Love herself had touched him that day.
He returned the stall to its owner-youth   *90*
And stealthily set off amongst the crowd,
Following them up the Acropolis:

> *Two women, who shall bedeck fair Dame Artemis;*
> *Hymen behind to worship his one true Mistress.*

PART THREE:
BRUSHING ALL THE WORLD

That night, Myiscus had an appointment
To meet Hymen at their favorite tavern.
This place of business lived on two levels:
Man's duties below, and woman's above –
With a godly shelf running vouchsafe 'tween.   5
The *House of Dionysos* was a bar
And place to grab food suitable for wine.
One large open space with a mezzanine,
Patrons coming in would find the master
Manning his counter of stone and of brick,   10
Submerged in which he kept various wines
Cooling out of the air in earthen vats.
When a client strode to the bar, he'd choose
Which grade of wine he could afford that day.
Grabbing ladle then, with a toothless grin,   15
The bar owner would start his idle chat,
Lifting away one of the wood covers
To pull out a draught of sanguine liquor.
With the motion of deft experience,
The wine airborne would become, only to   20
Gurgle in the buyer's cup with a splash.
Then it's up to the patron to decide
How much spring water – sitting around in
Pitchers on the counter – to cut his wine.

Foolish was he who drank condensed-wine straight, 25
And still more foolish not to pace himself
For the pleasant night of drinking to come.
During winter's months of cruel cold weather,
Charcoal-heated braziers lined the counters
For mulled cocktails, herbed and spicy bevies 30
In which wormwood and licorice root might
Keep hands and gullets warm on frosty eves.
It could also be known to melt the snow
From gray rooftops and re-ignite love's fire,
Stoked by shafts of Eros-kindling below. 35
While the barman plied the guests with his stock,
The wall behind contained the painted eyes
Of an all-protecting Dionysos.
The youth most godly lounged with his leopard,
As, standing by, with the boy's pinecone-tipped staff, 40
Seilenos his stepfather would watch.
Along the bottom of the gay icon,
An offertory shelf burned frankincense.
Placed either side stood honored souvenirs
From the god's shrine at holy Lerna town – 45
Life-sized fig wood 'members' of Prosymnus.
Also from this ledge hung gifts from patrons
In the form of Priapic charms and chimes
To bring youthful luck and vigor unto
The establishment, its owners, and guests. 50
On the mezzanine, cross-braced timber rails
Made for perfect views of the milling crowd,
While from behind her counter, food items,
Portioned and heated to order, kept folks
Sober enough to stay on imbibing. 55
Here the barkeep's missus had full control,
But when chores became too much, or dishes
Piled too high, needing thorough scrubbing,
Daydreams could grant temporary release.
And a look both content and faraway 60
Always accompanied idle chatter
Concerning that magic trip to Lerna.

Leaning against the second-floor handrail,
Myiscus paused, waiting for his buddy.
He raised a contemplative cup and drank –   65
His second of moderately good wine –
And then felt his stomach swim in hunger.
To his sharp mind not used to sophistry,
He could tie in this desire to bite
With the will to be bitten by love-lust.   70
Satiating the first, temporary;
Satisfying the second, a lifelong
Chase chaotic of the impossible.
"Is Myiscus tempted to love," he asked,
Scoffing, "like my fool friend Hymenaios?   75
No, not I…." He hesitated, turning
A bit weak, surprisingly, knowing why.
The insides of the young man rumbled then,
Smelling the aromas wafting from small
Pans and plates a-sizzle on the warming   80
Braziers behind where he pensively stood.
He swirled his drink, raising the cup over
His right eye; left still free to watch below.
"Maybe love is meant to be like hunger.
Perhaps the gods in their wisdom devised   85
One like the other for a good reason;
To let dim mortal consciousness conceive
One via the entrails of the other."
And thus Myiscus allowed full release
Of those warm thoughts he'd suppressed earlier.   90
Softly, he recited by memory
A note he'd received from Meleager:

    "For when the cock crows
    He merely rouses me
    To continue my weltering –   95
    Alone, on cold sheets,
    Myiscus is a dream.
    He seems meant to please and torment
    Both the night and day as equals."

Down front, a commotion rose from the door.
Myiscus stood tall, anticipating
Bright Hymen's appearance to end his gloom.
Instead, his warm smile got spilled on a group
Of tipsy, carousing guys coming in,
Obviously moving their party from
One of their parents' staid, private houses
To a public place where they could be as
Boisterous as their young, male hearts wanted.
The heart of Myiscus sank, for the last
Of the party in was Meleager.
They made eye contact. Myiscus turned cold,
And instantly saw a shadow of hurt
Pass over the poet's face beneath him.
The young man told himself he didn't care,
But as Meleager joined up and drowned
Within the group of his buddies, he thought
That at five years older than Myiscus,
Twenty-three was not 'old,' yet the poet
Carried more mature looks and gravity
Than any of his contemporaries,
Let alone all the teen boys he ogled.
Myiscus realized something startling:
"That guy just ogles one of us – that's me."
Much to his relief, Hymen entered then.
Myiscus waved his pal up, naturally
Attracting the unwanted attention
Of his would-be suitor, with his clear smile.
The young man went back; ordered right away –
He knew exactly what he craved to eat.
Myiscus grabbed a small table next to
The handrail overlooking the tavern.
Hymen came up, grabbed a stool and joined him.
He seemed to Myiscus to be glowing,
Even beyond his usual luminance.
Hymen cried forth: "I saw her today – I –
I actually got to touch her hand!"
"'Her' means Kathros?" Myiscus dared to ask.

"Yes! And I gave her a wreath of cypress
To offer to The Goddess Artemis,
But then I followed her to the hilltop.   *140*
Oh! Myiscus, you should have seen the grace
With which she trod every step of ascent,
Higher till she neared the red-veined altar.
How I wished to spring from my hiding place
And tell both the world and the gods alike   *145*
That I never want to leave Kathros' side!"
Myiscus murmured: "Is everyone mad,
Chewed on by blank verse and love poetry?"
Ignoring him, Hymenaios just smiled.
"And you know, I believe she felt it too.   *150*
Do you believe it happens at first sight…?"
Myiscus peered across the tabletop.
"So, now," continued Hymen, "I simply
Need to find how we can be together."
"Yeah," Myiscus chuckled. "That's all you need,   *155*
Never mind how impossible it is."
"Myiscus, pal, you need some faith, like me."
Fortunately for the darker young man,
His temper was cooled by the arrival
Of tempting dishes for them both to eat.   *160*
A steaming braise of taro in white wine
Clanged next to a saucer of deep-fried sprats.
Octopus minced with succulent chicken
Formed lovage-laced meatballs in pesto sauce.
And last to squeeze onto the tabletop,   *165*
Spelt rolls with oxyporum dipping sauce.[2]
From the hidden holster strapped to his thigh,
Hymen drew the dirk he always carried

---

[2] Oxyporum sauce: a concentrated base of dates and spices is diluted to taste with
white wine vinegar and fish sauce. To make the base, crack together 2 ounces
cumin with 1/2-ounce white peppercorns. Transfer to a food processor and add 1-
ounce fresh rue, an 1/8 of a teaspoon baking soda, about 12 pitted dates. Pulse
grind until mixed but still coarse. Drizzle in 4 ounces of honey and blend until
smooth. Store in a tightly lidded jar in the refrigerator and allow it to mellow a few
days. To use, put about a tablespoon of the base in a dipping bowl and mix in
about 1 tablespoon fish sauce to 2 tablespoons white wine vinegar (*de re coquinaria*,
I, [xviii]). For fish sauce, I prefer the light amber saltiness of Filipino *patis*.

45

To cut the potatoes in bitesize chunks.
They dug in, and blessèd silence followed   *170*
As the boys quenched at least half of their souls.
While chewing, Myiscus thought of 'a way,'
And joked rancorously with his buddy.
"I've given it some consideration.
The only method to spend some time with   *175*
The daughter of Stratos is to become
A girl yourself. In fact, then only if
You become like my sister, one of those
'Little cub bears' of the Artemis cult."
Laughter from Myiscus fell on deaf ears.   *180*
Hymen had stopped eating, his mouth grown large.
After he swallowed, he exclaimed brightly,
"That is the best idea you've ever had!"—
Hymen's blue eyes positively sparkled—
"Thanks, old friend, I just knew you'd help me out."   *185*
"I was joking! For you to be a bear,
You'd have to lose the things that make you male,
And *then* what's the point of having Kathros!"
Again, ignoring him, Hymen went on,
"It's a perfect plot, for in a few days   *190*
They will have their big procession, followed
By their annual pilgrimage on to
Artemis' temple in Brauron.
On their journey then I will tag along.
You yourself have said it often enough,   *195*
How I sometimes appear more like a girl,
So with wig and costume, I'll blend right in."
Myiscus asked, after swallowing hard,
"Have you gone nuts? You know what those women
Do to men who try to defile their rites"—   *200*
With his fingers, Myiscus made a snip—
"Well, they're your nuts! I guess you can decide."
To his surprise, Hymen merely chuckled,
Saying, "People can't waste their lives in fear
Never letting what they want take control.   *205*
At some point in time we must simply act."
A glimpse of someone's sad eyes flit across

Myiscus' conscience for a moment,
But it was lost when Hymen plainly asked,
"To make it work, I will need your help, friend."   *210*
Myiscus made reply with shaking head,
"I'll say you will! Someone has to shave you,
Including your legs!" Both boys chuckled then.
Still wagging his skull, Myiscus added,
"You *are* nuts but, they're yours to decide on."   *215*
The mezzanine lit up as Hymen smiled.
"Thank you, dear chum. After dinner, let's go
Back to your house and select clothes for me;
Hardly will your sister know they're missing."
As they resumed eating, Myiscus groaned: *220*
"One glance; one touch; and he's ready – snip; snip."
Hymen glibly chewed a taro morsel,
When from the floor below, boisterous cheers
Drew his interest to one within the group.
Grinning broadly again, elbows settling   *225*
Upon the tabletop, he repeated:
"It's all about seizing the day, my friend.
Not one of us is put on Earth to roam
Afraid of going for what we most desire."
Myiscus jeered, chin towards the handrail.   *230*
"Perhaps, but some of us could benefit
From being a little more circumspect."
Hymen seemingly changed the subject then.
"Did you ever notice the shrine shelf here?"
Myiscus laughed. "The pair of dildos? Those?"   *235*
"Yes, exactly! Do you know the story,
The faith behind that sacred love token?"
"No, but I have a feeling you'll tell me."
"Yes," Hymen said. "Dionysos wanted
To visit the underworld and retrieve   *240*
His mother's soul from the pyre Hara
Had reduced the god's mortal life-giver.
At the Alcyonian Lake, the teen met
Prosymnus who swore he knew the entrance
Via the lake to Hades, but since he'd   *245*
Many happy hours spent with the youth,

The price for the information was love;
For the two of them to marry one day.
Dionysos felt love for the man too,
But said he'd only return if his quest   *250*
Led his mother to Olympus as god;
If he could flee the horrid jaws of Hell.
Successful, the young man returned to learn
Of the Underworld's devious revenge:
Hades took Prosymnus to him in death.   *255*
Saddened his espoused was gone from the world,
The beautiful youth journeyed to his tomb,
And with the timber of a fig tree there,
Moistened the wood he carved with joyful tears
Into the member of his belovèd.   *260*
'Pon the mortal's grave, he consummated
The heaven-made match deemed never to die.
Thus the Boy-God returned to Olympus
Older, wiser and made fully a man.
That's why his worshipers still to this day   *265*
Will transition from ignorance to light
With the god's totem of undying love."
Myiscus summed up the story's moral:
"Even a single hour of love can
Transcend the grave's temporary nature.   *270*
With it, the soul will never need a tomb."
Hymen nodded. The darker boy absorbed,
But though the import dawned, he then still asked,
"And what made you think to tell me this tale?"
"The truth? Meleager's winning laurels   *275*
At last year's Dionysos Festival."
Myiscus smiled some, but dubiously.
"Ah, so that's the tie-in, but those awards
Were for poetry in praise of the gods.
The epigrams he hurls my way hardly   *280*
Seem worth writing down in ink, never mind
Carving in stone as a memorial."
The heat of trespassing his own feelings
Rose through him as a column of blushing.
Hymen ignored it and asked anyway,   *285*

"How is it you two came to meet at all?
I guess it wasn't at the gym, was it?"
"No, not at first. His family and mine own
Adjoining country properties and farms.
Eighteen months past, they agreed to a joint   *290*
Family picnic to honor Priapos
For bringing our orchards full of apples."
Myiscus heard his tone become softer.
"That was the day, and we had a private
Assignation away from prying eyes"—   *295*
Adamant Myiscus became, saying—
"How could I know it'd mean so much to him!"
Hymen's eyebrows rose in playful teasing.
"I have always thought that there was more than
Simple pursuer and pursued, and now,   *300*
Tonight, I have finally seen it clearly."
Myiscus protested on principle.
"Just 'cause love has painted your eyes prosy,
Don't go thinking you can whitewash others.
The whole world can't be brushed with your feelings—   *305*
You've been lured by Meleager's madness,
But have made it a type all of your own.
Next he'll be giving you lessons on how
Crazy love-epigrams should get written."
As the auburn boy merely smiled then,   *310*
Myiscus retorted, "Here. Tell me these
Strings of words are anything but madness:

        'If all my days are
        sadness,
        Why even live a day   *315*
        longer…?

        Carve this in stone? you may ask.
        Why not? I reply.
        Our hurts today
        Will still be hurts tomorrow.'"   *320*

49

Hymen continued to say naught, but by
The look of pain and joy both commingled
Upon his bright friend's face, Myiscus knew
Hymen found the words to be beautiful.
Myiscus wondered if not all poets   *325*
Were indeed nuts, as if full of the seed
Of godly madness, spreading this divine
Dissemination around on mankind.
His companion suddenly stood, saying,
"Come, let's go and start my transformation."   *330*
Myiscus laughed. "Yes, *my* insane idea.
How could I have forgotten it so soon?"
The boys went downstairs, and the bar section
Was packed, crowded and raucous, causing them
To loudly excuse themselves walking through   *335*
The assembly of glowing manliness.
Again, Myiscus made brief eye contact
With Meleager's sadness witnessed there.
As he and his friend drew near to the door,
Hymen and Myiscus stopped at a sound: *340*
Someone tinged a metal tray for silence.
When they glanced over to the bar, they saw
Two of his hale pals hoist Meleager
Up upon their rock-steady shoulder blades.
The poet's eyes locked onto Myiscus,   *345*
Causing every patron to do likewise.
Then with outstretched hands, and a clear voice, said:

    "I spent the whole night at the bar,
    submerging my pain at how he
    sends nothing but shivering looks   *350*
    raining down on me like winter.

    But wine can only heat so much;
    eyes not looking can't see beauty;
    and though lovely young men were there,
    a darkened chill enveloped me.   *355*

Thus afflicted, I left the bar
to feel Papa Zeus' warmth once more.
Myiscus is my sun to rise
with reviving hope every day."

Myiscus, dazed, amazed by the cheering
Of these strangers for but a stranger's love,
Felt moved but still unwilling to show it.

360

Hymen leaned close and whispered in his comrade's ear:
"That's how we should all go for what we hold most dear."

PART FOUR:
WITH LUCK AND BLESSINGS TOO

Upon the chosen day of festival,
Myiscus knew his wait was impatient,
Shuffling his feet, scanning the gathering
For his harebrained friend to make a debut –
But as what? That was all the mystery.   5
Myiscus lent a gown of his sister's,
Yet still nurtured hope Hymenaios would
See better of this folly and its peril.
Bright noise vied for his attention as he
So turned to see girls line up in the street.   10
Not alone yet, they patiently withheld
Griping sneers and eye-rolls for the preening
Their doting mothers and nurses bestowed.
Tears were one-sided, and so too the wails
Carrying "My little girl!" to the winds;   15
But in general, a holiday mood
Prevailed upon the crowd in welcoming ways.
Children giggled to see their teenage sis
Made up in finery; good food wafted
From the margins of the group where vendors   20
Hawked vittles while decrying rivals' food
As unfit for the goodness of the folks.
These, the most holy rites of Artemis,
Were reserved for girls just about to leave

Their homes, mothers and fathers, to go off   25
And live with a stranger in his own house.
But before investiture in marriage,
Before she had even met with a man,
The daughters of the city's high elite
Had chance to go on one ritual retreat –   30
With each other and a priestess to guide –
To discover the most guarded secret
Of what power her femininity
Possessed upon the workings of the Earth;
Of where it came, and to what it might lead.   35
For like a hibernating mama-bear,
This strength was asleep, but still vigilant
Within the breast of the full-grown woman.
In a young girl this power is more like
The coiled spring of a cub napping upon   40
The fresh-born grass of her golden summer.
The rites of the goddess were for the girl,
Her initiation to womanhood,
And her one chance to know prowess most strong
Before it slept again in matronhood.   45
'Mid the commotion, young Myiscus thought
The traditions for these sixteen-year-olds
Was similar to that for Cretan boys,
Although younger, they were 'kidnapped' by men
Arranged by families as best matches   50
To seduce the lad in the countryside
And teach the ways it means to be a man;
Obeyance and restraint chief amongst them.
Such a feeling Myiscus felt right now.
Not being made of stone, his heart could shift   55
Towards the one who professed love to him
And to the one who stoked his core within.
Slowly, sounds of the festival faded.
Myiscus, given to himself alone,
Smiled warmly thinking of Meleager.   60
So too a moment later – sounds returned –
He grew aware how the thought of the man

Roused his own hibernating cub downstairs.
"Sir, bestow a donation for our cause?"
A girl with her face half-hid by a veil   65
Jangled her open palm to Myiscus.
The boy, most embarrassed, put on the spot,
Replied, "You'll have to excuse me, young miss,
For I brought no coin with me here today."
The girl struck his shoulder with shocking force,   70
But laughed demure, closing her veil tighter.
"Stupid boy! Come you to such an event
With no votive to offer The Goddess?!"
"Well, I—"
       Her voice turned sweet, lashes flutt'ring.   75
"If you brought no gold, young man, silver'll do;
If no argent you possess, then copper
Will stand you a tiny favor from She,
The Great Artemis, favored like a man."
Myiscus blinked, stunned his catechism   80
Had omitted a startling fact about
The goddess of the dark woods and hunting.
While thus amazed, the brazen dame pinched him,
His cheek instantly sore from the assault.
"You may be dumb," she said, "but you're *quite* cute." 85
The obvious dawning upon him, he asked,
"Hymenaios, are you behind that scarf?"
"Lower your tone, young man." Hymen's real voice
Cautioned Myiscus' total surprise.
"But, buddy"—he stumbled—"you're beautiful."   90
And so his friend was in his sister's gown.
From his mother, Hymen borrowed a wig,
Which fair of color and comfy of fit,
Enhanced Hymen's fine, natural allure.
"Are you sure of this plan?" Myiscus asked.   95
"All our time," Hymen replied earnestly,
"Upon this dark Earth, as Sappho termed it,
Is wasted if not a moment's valor
Places us on our heart's valiant journey.
We must either try or prepare to die;   100
No other than these two choices have we.

Now, friend, please wish me luck on my attempt
To win me the heart of the girl I love."
Hand landing on Hymen's shoulder, he said,   25
"You go with my luck and my blessings too."
At that moment, a tinny trumpet's call
Heralded all the processional girls
To gather as one at the starting point.   30
People on the move, a shadow of doubt
Shaded Hymen's otherwise sunny face.
He took his buddy's arm while gesturing
To the muscleman seeming all in charge.
"Now," the boy said, "all I have to do is   35
Get past the guy who is taking down names,
Join the parade, and then, I'm home free."
Before his friend could protest and add more,
Hymen ratcheted up his falsetto.
"Or at least I will be past the first trial   40
Of my nascent maidenhood." He giggled,
Latching tighter and moving them along.
When they got to him, the man's "Name?!" question
Be-startled Hymen so, he locked in fear.
Now Myiscus, the ever best of friends,   45
Escorted the girl past, saying calmly,
"My sister, sixteen-year-old Hymena."
"Hold on!" he said. "Let me get a gander."
Obeying the command, the sweaty brute
To Myiscus' sense of prideful duty   50
Offended all he considered manly.
"Where ya goin', sweetheart"—the cad licked lips—
"Formalities first, you ripe little plum."
"Hymena," Myiscus replied. "Daughter
Of councilman Miletus and sister   55
To me, family heir and son."
"All right; all right." The grimy man wrote down
The relative details on his tablet,
Licking his lips again, eyes undressing
She cagy shy to his authority.   60
"Can't be too safe, little girl; some might try
To intrude and steal one of you himself."

56

He wiped his nose with his hand. "But you're clear!"
Myiscus planted his friend right next to
Kathros comforting her preening nursemaid,   65
For the girl sent 'way returns a woman,
And the maid's hankie accepted her tears.
With that, he disengaged their limbs to leave,
But Hymen pulled him back in for a kiss.
His cheek still hot from his buddy's bussing,   70
Myiscus heard: "Now take this thank you, for
No one has a brother more loving than me."
He left his companion and went to find
A place best suited to watch the parade.
All of the girls, eight of them in total,   75
Were lined up in two side-by-side columns.
Attendants and parents were shooed away
As the priestess of Artemis appeared.
While last-minute preparations were made,
The mind of Myiscus drifted a bit;   80
He wished the best for his friend but worried
An exposure might be the death of him.
Tingles on his neck made him lift his head
As if someone were keenly watching him.
Scanning the crowd only took a moment,   85
For a sad pair of eyes *were* locked on his.
Myiscus unguarded, before he knew
What he was even doing, sent a smile
Of solace sailing to Meleager.
Now the priestess was preparing to speak,   90
And once during the long drone of her words,
Myiscus happened to glance back and sigh.
His friends were still there, but Meleager
Had mercifully disappeared someplace.
Disappointment and relief fought in him…   100
But both disappeared a moment later.
For there by his side, several inches taller,
Had slipped the handsome young man and poet.
Clanging with trumpets' call stirred the crowd up,
And as shouts trailed behind them, the procession   105
Began its march towards Athena's Gate,

Beyond which the vast countryside opened.
A last worried look for his dear Hymen,
And Myiscus felt the swarm around him
Wander this way and that, about their day.   *110*
The blue poet could not be here ignored,
But in silence, Myiscus turned his gaze
And led Meleager to a hushed spot.
Twenty paces later they had arrived,
And both young men placed hands on the guardrail   *115*
Surrounding the city's white clocktower,
The Horologion – Tower of the Winds.
"Why do you like this boy, Meleager"—
The voice of Myiscus was plain and bare,
His gaze then holding onto the poet's—   *120*
"What makes me special somehow in your eyes?"
Meleager was tall, striking and bold;
His cinnamon-brown look revealed a soul
Too honest for this world of deceivers;
What one saw in the poet was sincere,   *125*
But the wavy mop of tan hair he met
Could do with a trim and expert combing.
It was all Myiscus could do not to
Pull the twenty-three-year-old down to him
And straighten him up now as the breezes   *130*
Transformed him into their boyish plaything.
"Why?" Meleager said. "Because…because –
You are always you. You never mislead;
You never dissuade, ridicule or lie.
And, you're beautiful, both inside and out."   *135*
Funny, Myiscus thought through amazement,
But those qualities are what the poet
Struck Myiscus to be in his thinking.
Almost as self-defense, he stammered out:
"But I'm no one unique; that much I know."   *140*
The poet moved to stand behind him, so
Myiscus leaned his back on the handrail;
The sun now as well as winds played sweet
With this sweet Meleager's wavy locks.
"I'll tell you, comrade dear, to me you are.   *145*

If you think I'm honest, then you must know
Every word of my epigrams speaks true
When of you they praise my profoundest love."
Despite himself, Myiscus shyly smiled;
No heart of stone was actually his.   *150*
Standing, he bid the other follow him,
And together started a leisured stroll.
They drew near the spot at the tower's base
Where the clockmaker placed an inscription.
Myiscus, feeling more secluded stopped,   *155*
Eyeing his would-be wooer with a grin.
"Tell," he laughed, "I bet when you were my age,
You had to beat off suiters with a stick."
Meleager smiled too. "How did you guess?"
"Look at you"—Myiscus tried not to tease,   *160*
For he was earnest—"who wouldn't want you;
So confident; blessed with intelligence—"
"And modesty," Meleager added,
Which made Myiscus laugh outright. "That too."
The happy young poet folded his arms,   *165*
Leaning his weight against the handrail
By the boy who had given him some hope.
"Do you know what the clockmaker inscribed?"
"No." Myiscus then shook his head, turning
To watch his potential tutor tell him.   *170*
"I think Andronikos Kyrrhestes said:

        'Help me, masons of the divine,
        Capture just one moment of life
        Written forever here in rock
        With the name of the boy I love.'"   *175*

At first, wide-eyed wonder from Myiscus
Proved how youthful and innocent he was,
But by slow survey of the poet's face,
He came to realize *he* was the subject
Of the spurious epigram quoted.   *180*
His reaction was that of a true boy,
For he stood and struck shoulder playfully

Against the earnest chest of the young man.
Then pulling his companion to his feet,
The two continued their leisurely walk.   *185*
Meleager, a fount of wisdom spoke
While gesturing up to the wingèd men
Personifying the eight-compassed winds.
These were in large relief below the roof
And featured life-sized, angelic figures,   *190*
Wings outspread in the full flight of breezes.
"Do you see, Zephyros is a naked youth,
His springtime bounty gathered in the folds
Of his slackened tunic off his body
To return warmth and goodness to the land."   *195*
Slowly rounding to a shady corner,
Meleager gestured to the next 'Wind.'
"But Boreas guards winter, that sad time
When hope sleeps and hibernation's a batch
Of hearts like mine who fear spring will ne'er come –   *200*
Do you wish to be the North Wind to me…?"
Myiscus stopped. That was a good question,
Because now he recalled how past actions
Had cast a wintry pall on his admirer
Who used to be so cheerful and funny.   *205*
"Do you expect me to change, just like that?
Meleager, to say I never cared
Would be like fooling me as well as you.
You are so wonderful—" Myiscus stopped,
Frightened by what he was about to do.   *210*
But now Hymen's words about being bold
Caused the dark boy to then extend his hand.
The poet, in shadowy disbelief,
Reached out and enveloped it in his own.
"My heart," Myiscus said, "is done sleeping.   *215*
No one has ever roused it like you do."
A sight almost too choice to be believed,
A speechless poet raised the beloved's palm
And kissed, slow tears like relief in his eyes.

* ~ * ~ * ~ * ~ * ~ * ~ * ~ * ~ * ~ * ~ * ~ * ~ *

Meanwhile, the dusty sunlight shone on the road 220
And its group of pilgriming young ladies
Marching merrily through the afternoon.
When they had arrived at the city gate,
Each novice to the will of Artemis
Had been given the means to camp the night: 225
A small bundle to sling upon her back –
Wherein parents had packed food for three meals –
And a taper to light once the sun set,
But whose length made for a good walking stick
Until such time as one end would be lit. 230
After the crowds had let them through the gate,
Signs of city turned into other sights;
A string of hamlets first, then open fields.
Past midday, the angled sun grew cooler
As travel-sore hours passed one by one. 235
And yet for Hymena, joy bounced her step,
Knowing she tread next to her dear Kathros;
In fact, she now realized happiness
Had never walked with her before today.
She stole a shy glance and quietly thought, 240
'What more is there to want upon the Earth,
Than the chance to love and have it returned.'
As they rounded a bend the road required
To hug the side of a grassy hillock,
The group's mistress pulled ahead a little, 245
Giving the tired girls some breathing room.
From behind Kathros and Hymena came
The chatty tones of a fellow wayfarer.
Because her voice was hushed so the leader
Would remain unaware from up ahead, 250
Kathros and Hymena bent open ears.
"Who knows what will happen to us tonight?!
I've been told we will be blindfolded,
Standing assembled against a cave wall,
And then, one by one, she'll take each of us 255
To strip, kissing her way down as she goes!"

Upon the same instant, Kathros and she
Who trod beside her left-hand side,
Turned to the girl with the startling intel.
The tattletale nodded her head quite strong,
Inviting the girl behind her to say,
"That's certainly *not* what I have been told.
A friend of a friend's cousin's sister said
We'll find in the Goddess' Grotto placed
The thing acolytes call the Sleeping Bear."
Into the dramatic pause, Kathros asked,
"What is this hibernating *ursa* then?"
"It is," the second girl confided low,
"The covered oaken dildo, of great size,
Carved in the shape of The Goddess' thumb."
The four girls were shocked, Hymena grabbing
Instinctively her veil to hide her blush.
"But what," inquired she, still quite shaken,
"Have we all to do with such a timbre…?"
The brazen girl in-the-know smiled and winked.
"After we're prepared," she said, "we must each
Deflower ourselves in *Her* holy rite.
Only upon her hibernating thumb
Will we learn of our feminine pleasures –
Before we wed a man; then it's too late!"
Kathros aghast, three pairs of eyes soon looked

> *Towards Hymena, who confirmed with her reply;*
> *A deep-set titillation exclaiming, "Oh, my!"*

PART FIVE:
LOVE, LIGHT OF THE WORLD

Itself too road-weary, the twilight sun
Rimmed the edges of the horizon gold,
But the deepening indigo of East
Inched overhead and allowed velvet drops
Of starlight to tuft their way through the gloom.   5
Kathros and Hymena, a cozy pair,
Indulged in their newfound intimacy
And led the way before their companions
Who griped vocally about conditions.
"Who knew," one asked, "the route would be so rough?"   10
"Yes," affirmed another, "my sandals slip
And slide beneath my feet with every step."
Kathros and Hymena exchanged quick nods,
Each daring the other to laugh out loud.
They held themselves back and, fortunate too,   15
For the third girl behind them then spoke up.
"Complain, complain, complain: that's all you do.
But look! Soon it will be dark, and before
The Dog Star has a chance to bark at us,
We'll be safely ensconced within the Inn   20
Upon Artemis' temple precinct."
"Then good," replied the initial missy,
"Because more than my feet hurting, I'm starved."
"At the holy inn, we'll find warming baths,

Hot-oil rubdowns by the priestesses too –
Followed by a meal with which we'll have wine."
"Not wine!" exclaimed the second young lady.
"Certainly wine, with our dessert table,
For by and by, you must sure remember
We're no longer girls, but full-fledged women."
"Sounds good," said the original speaker,
"But our leader should hurry: It's soon dark!"
While the three behind them kept chatting,
Hymena leaned close to her companion –
Her tone low and requesting confidence.
"Do you not feel like complaining as well?
The trail has not been nice to us today."
"True," said Kathros, "but growth's not easy, right...?"
All that's worthwhile in life must take effort."
"I could not agree more," chimed Hymena.
Kathros added, "I tend not to believe
In laws of man which stress duality –
That black must be the opposite of white;
That heat is the enemy of the cold;
That male is male, and female is female."
Astounded, Hymena let loose a smile.
"Your mind is so supple, my dear Kathros,
You should attend Academy lectures."
The girl then laughed sadly. "You speak as if
I or any young woman can intrude
On the philosophy chats hosted by men."
Color rose upon Hymena's visage.
"Oh, yes. I forgot; *we* aren't welcome there."
Such a comment had Kathros glancing deep
Within her companion's demurring pupils,
But to Hymena's relief, said nothing.
By way of distraction, Hymena said –
Pointing up to a particular star
Rising hard above the eastern hillsides –
"As if almost on cue, see that light come?
It's the blue-white star from the Virgin's folds:
The Ceres, or Spica sapphire of light."

"Yes, and so it is. One of heaven's gems."
"My mother always told me it's special,
And known to astrologers as two stars   *65*
Circling close in a binary orbit,
Showing us one face some days, and the next
Another side to its in-born beauty."
"How fascinating, and how lovely too."
"Yes, because of its nature, some say   *70*
Wingèd Hermaphroditos is she who
Guides the fair star in her path through Virgo."
Kathros gazed and said with admiration,
"Two but one still; united by difference,
Yet always true to who she's meant to be.   *75*
I envy her freedom and truth-telling.
For everyday lives, it's not so simple."
"Why do you say that, my lovely Kathros?"
"Think of it, Hymena; think how we are —
Held hostage to Man's conception of us.   *80*
Both his physical control and his mind
Makes of us unary prisoners to him;
Choice goddesses or whores; mothers or sluts;
Good or bad as if black or white opposed
The other, and did not complement it,   *85*
When the truth is, everything slips and slides,
Especially the fickle moods of Man!"
Nodding, Hymena could only agree.
"In fact," stated Kathros, "if I could be
Like one person in history, I'd choose   *90*
The founder of Holy Athens herself."
"Like Tiresias? Striking love-bound snakes
And then gender-changed from man to woman?"
"Yes, dearest Hymena. That's who I mean,
Because, imagine she of all mortals
Was more than wife and mother; more than stuck   *95*
Within a fixed body, for she was all.
She got to see just what the company
Of both male and female are truly like,
Privately, amid their ranks as equal."
Hymena blushed from forehead down to toes.   *100*

Kathros took note and chuckled openly.
"How lovely," she said, "is your modesty.
Your shy coloring reminds of a quote
Thymocles is recorded as saying:

> 'You remember, I trust –   105
> You of all people remember
> When I recited this holy verse
> To you: "Beauty is fairest,
> and beauty is nimblest."
>   110
> Not the reddest bird
> in the sky shall outstrip
> beauty. Look, now,
> how all your blossoms
> are shed to the earth."'[3]   115

Hymena blushed yet deeper, but replied,
"I could not agree more, my kempt Kathros!"
Meanwhile, the party of marching women
Together pooled at one spot on the road;   120
Their leader and guide had gathered them there.
"Now, girls," she then announced, "here are tapers,
As we've yet another half-hour to trek.
One will be lit, and then step you forward
To ignite your own most precious flambeau."   125
So said, a spark was struck, and the first light
Illuminated the leader's visage.
As others came to get and strike torches,
Points of light slowly encircled the group,
Because the girls – kissed by the leader's flame –   130
Took positions round the perimeter
While others waited in line for their chance.
Hymena and Kathros seemed to be last,
But neither minded their time spent alone.
Hymena twinkled as she told her mate,   135
"Before you quoted about modesty;

---

[3] Thymocles' poem: *Greek Anthology* 12.32, translation after Paton.

But here, let me cite one Meleager,
A heart-sick bard who worships my brother:

> 'The Boy God of Love is the world's best source
> To enlighten our days, and lead our ways.'" 140

Thus it became Kathros' turn at flushing.
Though the eyes of every girl watched their guide,
Hymena's could only see her Kathros,
Whose smile made the rest of the world her prop. 145
Finally – their chance to come to get some light –
Hymena reached out and took both tapers.
Holding them wedged together, she got
One spark to ignite both of their flambeaux.
Kathros reached to take hers, but Hymena 150
Then asked, "May I hold this light for us both?"
Kathros puzzled. "I'm more than capable—"
"I know you are, but can't you see, dear girl,
As surely as the stars rotate at night,
In life I'll always carry a torch for you." 155
Before Kathros could speak, growling sounded
From the darkness outside the girls' circle....
Flick'ring shadows revealed approaching forms.
The group now grew smaller; steps taken back
Tried to ensure safety within numbers, 160
But screams arose, because upright black bears
Mewed loudly and lunged for the young women.
Tapers dropped as some were grabbed and detained.
Wild thoughts in Hymena's head wondered if
This was part of the initiation – 165
Ursa being sacred to Artemis –
But such dreams ceased the moment their leader
Was nabbed and gagged by another two bears.
One held the struggling woman from behind –
Her taper burning helpless on the road – 170
While the other laughed and used his paws to
Lower the grizzled bear mask from his head.
No servants of the Goddess were these brutes,
But Hymena saw they were beastly men:

Uncouth; unclean of both minds and actions.   *175*
This unmasked one proved to be their top dog,
For the marauder whistled sharply then,
Drawing all attention to his shouting.
"Make it easy on yourselves, princesses –
You spoiled daughters of the rich and powerful –   *180*
For you're our captives now, till your daddies
Cough up the gold to have you safely back."
The still-masked goons pointed noses upwards
And howled like hyenas giddy at blood.
Four of them, plus the leadman, gathered close,   *185*
Rustling the frightened young women like sheep.
"Come 'long, you little cubs of Artemis,
We have a secure cave to hole up in
While the ransom demands are carried out."
Treading o'er the road once more, Hymena   *190*
Considered options, but for now played dumb;
Patience would expose the kidnappers' faults,
And through such fractures, a plan could be made.
Coolness was called for, so she'd bide her time,
But Kathros stayed her chief priority.   *195*

> *Although an increased heartrate called her to action,*
> *The strap round her thigh gave pausing satisfaction.*

PART SIX:
IN THE CAVE OF MAN

The marauding band of rogue kidnappers
Had plied their assailant plans carefully,
Tracking the route the pilgrim young ladies
Took till a bend in the road and darkness
Gave them opportunity to don fur   5
And spring with the element of surprise.
They had taken them to a secret cave
Previously outfitted with the goods
For the girls' comfort, and their own vices.
Blankets would warm females through the long night,   10
While alcohol stood by to heat the men's
Potentially flagging courage with draughts
From pendulously large goatskin bottles.
Now most of them sat near the cave's entrance,
Pouring one another potable strength   15
With loud oaths, laughter, and crotch-grabbing boasts.
Their shifty eyes passed over the firelight
Of a central pyre of burning flambeaux
To ogle the young women held captive.
Belches and tipped backsides to let rip gas   20
Did the male of the species no credit –
In the eyes of their lady observers.
The girls huddled in groups of two and three,

Conversing in soft, reassuring tones,
That all would resolve itself for the best,   25
That friends and family would rescue them.
In mirror of their need for security,
Most pulled their blankets near while they bunched close,
Drawing the rough wool up to shoulder blades.
Hymena glanced furtively to the men   30
And watched the girls' leader where she sat;
The brutes had knocked the woman unconscious
When they abducted them back on the road.
Now the guardian priestess stayed quite still,
Gripping trembling girls on each side of her   35
And sputtering soothing sounds from her lips.
Close to Hymen's right side was Kathros,
So she raised an arm and pulled the girl in,
Resting a hand on Kathros' upper arm.
And shifting their shared blanket higher up.   40
"Are you warm?" she asked, holding the girl's eyes.
"Yes, Hymena. I'm comfortable. Are you?"
Drawing Kathros a bit closer, she smiled,
Indicating without words she felt well.
Hymena dared to lift her fingers and   45
Lovingly caressed Kathros' dark hair.
The other girl sighed, letting her eyes close.
Emboldened thoroughly by modesty,
Hymena guided the girl's head to hers,
And gently kissed the pale flesh of her lips.   50
Kathros then opened her eyes to a squint
As if sav'ring Hymena's precious gift.
A moment later, she returned the kiss,
Smiling her way through a fog of warming…
But then the young girl stopped and drew away.   55
Hymena trailed the sightline of concern
Emanating from her companion's gaze,
And spied the causing source of her withdrawal –
The abductors' loutish top dog watched them,
Wiping his goonish mouth after some wine   60

With the grease-smeared, hairy back of his hand.
"Don't worry about him," Hymena said,
Pulling Kathros tighter to her again.
"We're safe as long as we stick together."
Eventually, Kathros relaxed again,   65
Allowing Hymena to feel the girl's
Reassuring weight, once more as her head
Came to rest upon her sturdy shoulder.
"Hymena, oh, tell me it is not true."
"Tell you that what is not true, dear Kathros?"   70
The young girl's eyes tracked to their kidnappers.
"That we in marriage must be given to
Men no better than animals, like these."
As if on cue, from the distracted men,
Belches couched in crude laughter rent the air.   75
Hymena drew her belovèd closer.
"Concern yourself not with such examples
Of how low the male of our genus crawls,
For some are noble and will surrender
All to protect the ones they hold most dear."   80
"I meant"—Kathros hesitated somewhat,
Turning her eyes to meet those of Hymena—
"The love from woman to woman is sweet:
It's not belittled through competition,
Not tested through prodigious feats of strength,   85
Not garnished, chipped away by jealousy.
It can stay pure, unchanged and unchanging
Across the years and above many trials."
Hymena slowly nod her head. "It's true,
For your words contain great wisdom, Kathros,   90
And I'd need to be a god to dispute
What our eyes evidence to us daily:
Love 'mongst women is a beautiful thing."
"I doubt," Kathros said with more conviction,
"Men can feel this level of tenderness   95
With one another, let alone a girl."
Hymena grinned. "You still have much to learn,"

But changed the course of the conversation.
"Speaking of love, Kathros, tell me about
How relations are with your family. 100
Have you siblings to love with your parents?"
As if in hesitating slow motion,
Kathros raised her head and sat very still.
"I have Father and Mother, and my nurse –
They all love me very much, but it's Nurse 105
Who dithers and frets the most after me.
I am sure this evening finds her worried,
But hopefully she knows not yet I'm lost,
Abducted, locked in a dingy cavern."
"It sounds like she is very protective." 110
A slight flicker of a grin played about
The lovely lips of Kathros. "Oh, she is.
I'm sure she'd want to separate us too."
Hymena felt a blush creep up her neck.
"She would? And why would she seek to do that?" 115
Kathros shrugged. "Because I am her baby,
And especially…after…. Well, I mean,
Nurse wants no harm to befall me, ever."
Kathros brightened a moment. "And with you,
Hymena dear, what of your family? 120
Tell me all about your domestic life,
For your dear Kathros wants to learn it all."
Within her own thoughts, Hymena scrambled,
Then she recalled how her wily best friend
Was not only kith, but her kin as well. 125
"Like you, I have Mother and Father too,
But also, a twin brother, Myiscus."
"Oh, Hymena – brothers are a great joy."
Although her words were happy, Hymena
Saw only sorrow on Kathros' visage. 130
Her instincts were to comfort, and reached out
To bring Kathros into resting contact
Within the bolstering circles of her arms.
She did, much to Hymena's great relief.

"It is blessed to have a brother to love,   *135*
And Myiscus is a dear friend as well –
He and I harbor no secrets at all
As unworthy of sharing between us;
We have a love that cannot be questioned."
"Hearing this, Hymena, fills me with both   *140*
Gladness for you and sorrow for myself."
"Yes, Kathros, but why should be that the case?"
"It is so, because when you asked before
If I had either sisters or brothers,
I avoided answering with the truth.   *145*
You see, I once had a younger brother,
But he died in my thirteenth year of life."
"I am saddened to hear of that, Kathros."
"It was the moment I was invited
By my mother and aunts – my relatives –   *150*
To full womanhood and do our duties
As a home bequeathed his sad obsequies."
"That is a young age to be called upon,"
Said Hymena, stroking Kathros' hair,
"To function as a woman of the house.   *155*
If you'll permit an indelicacy,
You can tell me what happened, if you want."
Kathros steeled herself to relive the day
Tragedy stalked her entire family.
"At a picnic held far in the country,   *160*
The adults lunched under the olive trees,
While Nurse, my brother and I wandered off.
We found a shaded stream gurgling with life,
And we two children went in for a swim.
The water was too cold; too deep also.   *165*
Eventually, my brother's remains turned
Up on a rocky sandbar in the river.
It was the worst day I have ever lived...."
"Oh, my Kathros, I am sorry for you.
You are too young to have known such sorrow."   *170*
The girl turned her warm eyes on Hymena.

"Treasure your brother. I miss mine each day."
Wondering if it would lighten the mood,
Hymena asked, "Shall I tell you of him?"
"Yes, please. It would be wonderful to hear."   *175*
Hymena chuckled. "Well, first, he's quite brave;
Will stand up to any bully out there,
And he nurtures for himself honesty,
Except in one area."
                            "Which is that?"   *180*
"See, Myiscus is loved by a poet –
One divinely possessed Meleager,
Who never fails to fill the air with love
For the boy he loves more than his own life.
I speculate Myiscus secretly   *185*
Returns the poet's passion, but for now
Is too proud to let himself be wooed thus.
But my brother is a bit of a fool
To deny he's already fallen now."
"Well, yes. I know, brothers can be stubborn!"   *190*
Both laughed, and in their laughter and sharing,
Felt the bond cement and draw them closer.
Encouraged, Hymena picked up her hand
And nearly choked up, asking her Kathros,
"Tell me, please – have you ever been in love?"   *195*
Kathros slightly stiffened. "Laugh at me not,
But you believe in love at first sight…?"
"I do. I know it happens every day."
"I have felt it, Hymena. I felt it."
"Felt it for whom…?"   *200*
                            "It was for a stranger –
One who's sure to be a demigod son
Of brazen Helios, sun god himself."
Hymena began to feel her heart race.
"And where did you chance to meet this bright boy?"   *205*
"Selling his garlands in the Agora,
And I confess, the moment he touched me,
I felt sparks pass between our ling'ring hands,

One I have only sensed one other time."
Kathros played with Hymena's slim fingers,   *210*
Confirming in seductive tones belief:
"As good as the other may be, it is
Same-sex love that's nobler simply because
It merges absolute social equals.
It is not saddled with societal   *215*
Hogwash about roles; it can simply be.
Yes, Hymena, I envy your brother
And the love he receives from his poet."
"But who, Kathros, was this one other who
Inspired love in you at first contact?"   *220*
Risen once more to face her, Hymena
Could see a bittersweet expression rise
Upon the features of his kempt Kathros.
"Actually, Hymena, you remind me
Of that youth at the flower stand a lot."   *225*
"I do...?"
          "Oh, yes, and much more than that too."
"Too? And too, what?"
                    "And you too make me feel..."
"Make you feel love?"   *230*
                    "Yes, you fill me with love."
Such news should have wakened Hymena heart,
But instead, she felt the weight of the lie
Come between them, and must rectify it,
Despite potential, dire consequences.   *235*
She held Kathros' eyes. "Though same-sex love
Is indeed nobler, love twix the sexes
Can aspire to the same high level;
It can oft do and dare like the heroes."
Kathros merely appeared to be puzzled.   *240*
"What if," Hymena continued softly,
"You could meet just one love-enamored boy
Who'd risk all to be near the girl he loved?"
"I don't understand your words, Hymena."
"Do you think you could give your heart to this   *245*

One, desperate, crazy boy who'd risk his life
To sneak into – oh, I don't know – an all
Girls' rite of passage in a borrowed dress?"
Confusion turned somewhat curt, Kathros asked,
"What on earth are you rambling on about?" 250
"I mean, say this boy just wanted to spend
A few, innocent, blissfully slow hours
Merely to be by your side, just to hear –
I mean, if I *were*…. I say, if I *had*…"
Hymena stumbled in her own persona. 255
"Oh, the gods be blessed, and just look at this."
She demurely opened her gown a bit,
Exposing truth to her identity.
Kathros was shocked. She pushed herself away
And managed to stand in time to collide 260
With the drunken leader of the kidnappers;
His eyes were hazy in the film of lust.
"Well, well," he said, pushing Kathros back down.
"Have our Sapphatic sisters had a tiff?"
Hymena's eyes sought the priestess for help; 265
The woman rose, but the rest of the goons
Followed suit, and restored the *status quo*.
The top dog's wine-soaked, gurgling words then said,
"There's nothing I like to see less than two
Pretty young girls engage in a catfight." 270
He sat between them then, lifting his hands
To lock each in place by smelly armpits.
Hymena glimpsed fear in Kathros' visage;
She gestured to stay calm and play along.
As expected, the lecherous man turned 275
His sloppy attentions to Hymena.
"What's-a-madder, you stupid, sexy thing –
You no-likey the interest of real men?"
Hymena clutched her veil, slapping him hard,
And before the brute could react, sang-song: 280
"Heavens, no! I belong to Artemis!"
The kidnapper, rubbing his now-sore cheek,

Gave up and shifted his lust to Kathros.
"What about you, honey, you ain't like men?
Believe me, you don't know what you're missing." 285
He gestured vaguely down. "I got the fella
You just gotta meet. Let me intro you,
'Cuz he just loves handshakes from pretty girls."
Kathros opened her mouth to reject him,
But that proved to be too much stimulus. 290
He yanked her shoulder and dove for her neck,
Lips wetly groping the flanks of her skin.
Her fists flew and started punching his chest.
The thug brought round his arm from Hymena
And started to pin Kathros by the wrists, 295
His panting slobber coming more quickly
As the delicate girl struggled 'neath him.
Kathros let out a desperate scream, and then
Got a shock, as the ugly man screamed too.
He yelled again, writhing away from her; 300
Stumbling to his feet, his hands feeling his back.
Hymena stabbed again, this one finding
And ripping open his heart. The dead man
Dropped with a thud on the cave's callous floor.
With venom, Hymena addressed the corpse: 305
"I told you, *we* belong to Artemis."
The other hoods came run towards her;
Hymena spun, wielding the bloody knife,
Commanding them "Stop!" with booming echoes.
The ruffians halted like scared schoolboys. 310
Hymena told them with ominous calm,
"Artemis commands thee to halt thy course.
Dare not to make Her angrier than this,
Or She'll quick turn you into female bears.
Though only slightly more savage than now, 315
You would have merely wild berries to lick
And know intimately what brutal rape
At the hands of some heartless beast feels like,
Only your foul screams will be heard by you.

As none but you can hear inside your head,   *320*
You'll have no voice to let loose your sorrow."
Hymena added with deepening ire,
"Such things happen to men who dare to spy
On Dame Artemis and Her young ladies."
The rascals felt their middle leg contract....   *325*
Hymena took deep breaths. "Out!" she shouted.
The men screeched, tripping over each other
To get out of the cave. Into the woods
Each found his direction and ran like fire.

In truth, they never looked behind to goad that prof,[4]   *330*
Lest the Mighty Goddess should snip their manhood off.

---

[4] Prof – profanation; a defilement.

PART SEVEN:
LOVE SANCTIFIED

After the men had fled, a great cheer flowed
Through the young women jumping to their feet
And surging towards where Hymena stood.
At the same instant, Kathros threw her arms
Around the neck of their liberator,   5
Only she knowing though of whom she hugged –
The rest thought they saw mortal girl embrace
Divine incarnation of Artemis.
Excitement and questions moved Hymena
To open her mouth and inquire if   10
The actions of Kathros signaled requite
For feelings she's admitted earlier.
As the words of "If...if...." formed upon her lips
But before any more could be uttered,
The high priestess tossed a blanket over   15
The lifeless corpse of their defeated foe,
And curtsied herself on a single knee
Before The Goddess' holy presence.
"Bow, bow," said she. "All of you girls kneel down
To honor our blessings from Artemis."   20
At that word, Kathros tried pulling away,
But Hymena – catching onto her waist –
Kept the young woman standing by her side.

Bidding with gesturing hand, Hymena
Encouraged everyone to rise once more. *25*
Yet, no one paid the 'goddess' any mind,
Which as far as humans go, is usual.
Inside, Hymena was in a quandary,
For now that she'd revealed her affections,
Which Kathros seemed to suggest were returned – *30*
But lacking chance to check it vocally –
Hymena grew vexed to consider how
Myiscus had warned her to be wary.
The cult could turn the very weapon used
To secure their liberty upon her, *35*
And rob her of that asset yet hidden.
"I'm not," the still-veiled Hymena began
Timidly quaking in every word,
"That which my outward manners might bespeak.
For no goddess I; much less a woman. *40*
I'm just an inferior youth compared
To all the female prowess in this cave,
But I perpetrated this hoax with one
And only one motivation in mind."
She drew Kathros a bit tighter to her *45*
And in her beloved, dreamy expression
Waxed as poetical as a moonbeam –
"For you see, I'm a humble boy who fell
In love with a girl high above my rank.
In me you see a pebble stone gazing *50*
At the bright orb of Aphrodite through
The too-swift moving waters of a brook.
From my place on the riverbed I hoped
She'd fall a shooting star, down by my side,
Or wished a god would place me up by her – *55*
Although unworthy for her firmament."
Kathros gently picked up Hymena's hand,
Saying, "Either ascended from earthy
Trivialities to the height of stars,
Or fallen from the divine to the ground, *60*

There is no part of me that loves you not.
I'll love *you*, no matter when, where or guise:
Male, female, or the both – boy, girl, or none –
I give my heart eternally to yours."
Slowly, Kathros and Hymena leaned in,   65
About to consecrate their new union
With a sacred, vow-affirming kiss, when
The group's leader suddenly cleared her throat.
Stumbling to her feet, the priestess stepped close,
And all the other young women stood too.   70
After taking that step, a priestly hand
De-wigged Hymena's head, revealing
The boyish haircut of the auburn youth.
One girl from the crowd walked up and announced:
"That kid I know! He's one of my brother's   75
Associates at the Lyceum, but –
But to tell the truth, I think this redhead's *weird…*"
Shocked cries from the girls circled the cavern.
"Is that my dress?! Oh, my god, he *is* weird!"
And Hymena quickly tried to explain,   80
"It was merely for love of my Kathros
That I hid myself amongst your numbers.
I never had any mind to…. Defile…."
Hymena gulped, sound coming out of her
Faint, yet too-terribly insipid grin.   85
"Now that you've ruined it, you can keep the dress."
Hymena's third leg retracted a bit
As the bold priestess stared him in the eye;
Hymena could not tell what the woman's
Stern and chiseled, expressionless face   90
Bode for his future and integrity.
Slowly, that featureless mouth rose a smirk,
And the cleric turned to the assembly.
"The Fates," she announced boldly, "have blessed us.
The gods and the most Holy Goddess have   95
Deemed fit to save us, through this young couple."
The leader gazed on Hymena and Kathros

And smiled as radiantly as the sun.

"*For now that you our would-be bullies did outwit,*
The Goddess shows She loves your love and sanctifies it."   *100*

PART EIGHT:
SOARING

Hoisting aloft to gain a bird's-eye-view,
The road's dark green foliage of summer
Shimmered merrily through the midday heat.
The tight band of acolyte Little Bears
Chatted, making their way back towards town; 5
Fatigued, the girls were also jubilant.
From her regal position out in front,
The high priestess led with newfound vigor.
Following close in her train was Kathros
And the re-wigged and re-veiled Hymena, 10
For better to be guised as all woman
Than either male or female in disguise.
Meanwhile, back in town, the Agora buzzed
In swarming conference circles comprised of
The male relatives of the kidnapped girls 15
Talking out their options for the ransom;
Although the bright light of Helios shone
Upon their visages, their hearts were dark
With fear for the safety of their daughters,
Sisters, cousins, nieces – all in danger. 20
The sire of fair Kathros was arguably
Just as stoic as the rest, but perhaps
In his heart of hearts, more deeply afraid,
As he loved his daughter like the treasure

All so readily admitted she was.
Off to the side, but with a perfect view,
Meleager and Myiscus stood by,
Watching the ever-shifting scene of talk.
As well as his dear best friend, Myiscus
Had his sister among the hostages,
Making him anxious to be doing more.
The poet gently grasped his hand, shaking
Myiscus out of his fixed reverie.
"Meleager, I want to take up arms
And strike out to find them. There's too much talk
And too little action to suit my tastes."
"I know, my bold Myiscus, because when
The conferring fathers and relatives
Decide that a search party is called for,
You and I, and all of this poet's friends,
Will be the first out of the city's gates;
This I pledge, along with my life, to you."
Hearing his belovèd's unadorned words
Boosted the spirit of Myiscus, so
He tightened his hold on the poet's hand,
Thanking him without any need of words.
While they were thus engaged in confidence,
Motion attracted the eyes of both men,
For the nursemaid of Kathros was there too.
This determined woman buzzed the outside
Of the groups of huddled elders like an
Excited hummingbird – all a flutter
Of arm, veils and tears. A flurry of sound
Escaped her mouth in the manner of wings
Flapping quicker than human perception
Could normally make out by observing.
"Look there," Meleager said, gesturing,
"See how she bravely circuits the outside
Of the talking men like a *kolímpri.*"
"You're right," laughed Myiscus. "A hummingbird,
Unafraid to stop and stare a mere man
Dead in the eyes: her wordless fretting says

Time's a-wasting! to the dithering males.
"She's not alone in this anxious feeling"—
Myiscus slightly raised his partner's hand   *65*
To place a kiss on the poet's knuckles—
"You, Meleager, may want to be first
In the search party's vanguard, but beware –
You'll probably have to fight that woman
To even get out of the city gates first!"   *70*
The poet laughed, returning his boy's kiss.
"I've no doubt, but love is love after all;
As long as we're striving for the same goal,
Hers remains as valid as yours and ours."
The dear price of exhaustion came to him,   *75*
And Myiscus walked into his man's embrace
Relishing the comfort of the poet's arms
Gently surrounding him, placing his head
On Meleager's chest to hear his heartbeat.
The older caressed the younger man's back.   *80*
"Even through uncertainty and worry
About Hymen, your sister and the girls,"
Crooned Meleager lightly, "I must say
You've made me the happiest man on Earth."
Myiscus pulled back just enough to hold   *85*
The dreamy gaze of his belovèd's eyes.
Teasingly – already knowing the answer –
Myiscus inquired, "So, now poet,
You'll say my love has made all the difference?"
"Oh, yes – all the difference. Whereas before   *90*
My soul ached from the growing of its wings,
With you it now soars above the mundane,
Happy to stretch along with your spirit
Upon the warm currents of love aloft."
Laughing, Myiscus jokes good-naturedly   *95*
"Oh, what a burden to love a poet!
But I do love you; love you as I love
This existence, and now can't imagine
It going on without you in my life."
Slowly, Myiscus rose on his tiptoes,   *100*
And their lips came together for a kiss.

Lost together then for timeless moments,
Behind their closed eyelids and conjoined souls,
Gradual sounds of cheers penetrated.
As they could tell it swelled like a sea wave   105
Coming their way through the city.
Suddenly, small children burst into the square.
Their lips at first formed incoherent words,
But soon joined in a combined cheer: "They're free!"
Immediately trailing them, a throng   110
Poured into the Agora from a street
Leading directly from the Timepiece Gate.
The applauding grew as the high priestess
Came leading Artemis' acolytes
Into the city's main gathering place.   115
First to swim through the abysmal people,
Kathros' nursemaid located her young charge
And hugged the stuffing out of her, but then –
Turning slowly red – she buzzed like a hornet,
Stinging mad at how she had worried her.   120
In a minute more, all the girls were nabbed
By their servants, brothers and concerned friends.
Getting to the marketplace's center,
The small band of un-kidnapped pilgrims stopped.
Amid the noise and buzz then, one by one,   125
The much-relieved fathers of the young girls
Made their way to their respective daughters.
Up to Kathros, Hymena and the maid,
The young woman's progenitor arrived.
He smiled, hugging her from outright relief.   130
"Kathros, your mother is beside herself
Back at home with worry." He grabbed her wrist.
"We must tell her the good news right away!"
Without much effort, Kathros resisted
The adamant tugging of her father,   135
And after having extracted her arm,
Placed her hand lovingly in Hymena's.
The fidgety nanny cast aspersions
On this public display of affection.
Myiscus and Meleager arrived   140

86

With the young man's younger sister in tow.
Kathros' father, then realizing
He'd forgotten to ask the story, said,
"How came it to pass that all of you girls
Managed to escape your captors unharmed?"   145
Myiscus' sibling chortled loudly,
Saying, "Oh, no. This will be quite a show!"
At the promise of spectacle, the nurse
Elbowed her way around Meleager
To stand in front of the tall young poet   150
Who had dared to formerly block her view.
While the question from her father lingered
Still in the air, Kathros cast a shy glance
Into the clear eyes of her belovèd.
Hymena was just about to speak when   155
The high priestess burst on the little group.
Her hand landed upon Hymena's arm –
"By a heaven-sent miracle, good sir,
One blessed by no one less than The Goddess."
Excited now and intrigued, the father   160
Repeated for anyone to tell him:
"What happened? Explain how you got away."
"She saved us, Father, by her bravery;
Hymena alone stood up to those men
And kept me from the fate that's worse than death.   165
She pulled a dagger and stabbed their leader,
Killing him, causing the others to flee
'Fore a single girl's virtue could be harmed."
Kathros' father, a truly gen'rous man,
Proudly strode up to Hymena, and then   170
Announced so the whole company might hear,
"I humbly thank you, and say that you may
Have anything I keep possession of."
Hymena, in spite of herself, blushed pink;
What else in this situation could she   175
Think to say since this opportunity
Opened up before her like a flower.
"Love's bright," started she most tentatively,
"And where nothing was before, it can make

Man from a boy and woman from a girl.   *180*
From the dull purposelessness of living,
Make a being who knows why they were meant
To live a life where they'll only die.
From the rules of chaos, only love stands
Above them all, as the absolute rule   *185*
Against which existence's suffering
Can be measured. Alone, love can create."
She turned her words on the general crowd,
Catching the anxious glint in the nurse's scowl.
"I hid among your daughters and sisters   *190*
Not because I sought the better of them"—
She glanced into the eyes of her Kathros—
"But because my newformed heart keeps its
Better half within Kathros' radiance."
She continued to the young girl's father,   *195*
Noting Nurse was hyperventilating,
"For that reason, I sought to be near her;
To secretly breathe her in all unknown,
For I love her more than words can define.
Please sir, with Kathros' consent, grant that we   *200*
May spend the ages of life as spouses."
And with this, Hymena genuflected
Before the girl's father to await
The verdict of Fate to be cruel or kind.
All too much, trauma overcame her heart   *205*
And the nursemaid fainted with a whinny
Straight into the pert arms of the poet.
At this point, Hymena realized she'd
Forgotten to unmask her false disguise.
While the hushed crowd split intrigued glances twix   *210*
Kathros, her father and the girl knelt down
A supplicant before him, Hymena
Hastened to add, "But, sir, please be assured
The virginity of no one was lost,
And that also happens to include mine!"   *215*
The priestess vouched for the cosmic blessing.
"This union's sanctified by Artemis,

The Great Goddess herself, please keep in mind...."
The poor progenitor, what could he do?
Although he'd had hopes for a marriage to   *220*
A fine upstanding man of the town,
Love's love, and no father stands in its way,
Even though what's being asked of him is
His most precious possession on dark Earth.
He lifted Hymena to eyelevel,   *225*
Inquiring plainly of his daughter,
"And you return the love of this person?"
"Yes, more than any other part of life."
"Well, then," he said, jostling Hymena's neck,
"Wait till your mother sees who you're bringing home,   *230*
But I'll not stand in the way of true love,
Especially not one so heaven-matched!"
Romance was young again, and people sighed
Remembering the thoughts of their first love.
Desperate to be rejoined, Meleager   *235*
Transferred the still-blacked-out and groggy maid
For Myiscus' sister to support.
The boys came together to hug and kiss.
Hymena and Kathros likewise drew close,
Clasping hands and sweet eyes at the center   *240*
Of the people waiting and cheering them.
Just as the lips of the two young ladies
Came together to seal their betrothal,
The maid roused to her senses, gazing up.

> *Seeing Kathros and some pretty girl kissing then,*   *245*
> *The hefty woman fainted dead away again!*

PART NINE:
THE BEST OF FRIENDS

Some friends, the night previous the wedding day,
Feasted Hymenaios in his own house
As was the custom before the new bride
Entered the home she'd eventually rule.
Following the First Table, came dessert.   *5*
The honey-laced confection were arrayed
Before the three couches on the table,
Well within relaxed reach of the diners.
Hymen, Myiscus and seven more friends
Lounged then and laughed freely to the wee hours.   *10*
Along with the sweet course, servants hauled in
The large *krater* of bronze – four boys alone
Needed to bring it into the dining room.
It was freshly stocked with cool spring water
From which ladlesful would be mixed with wine   *15*
And served to the uproarious bachelors.
As was the custom, the boys got tipsy,
Knowing they could spend the night where they were,
Free from the worry of finding their way home
Drunk in the midst of a night turned morning.   *20*
About the second hour after midnight,
The wine stewards too – handsome lads themselves –
Were invited onto the couches to nap,
Some foot play, both innocent and not so,

Going on between the waiters and patrons.   25
In another hour, all were asleep
Except best friends Hymen and Myiscus
On the cushioned central couch of honor.
Slowly with care, the young men rose to stand,
The banquet a warm glow in their stomachs,   30
And exited as quietly as mice.
They headed towards the refreshing sounds
Coming from the wide-open main garden
With its fountain in motion night and day.
Upon the grass both cool and inviting,   35
The boys once more came to a settled rest
Lying flat on their backs – heels kicked up on
The curbs of the gurgling water feature –
They gazed up at the stars, folding their hands
Over their chests, and chatting like only   40
The best of friends feel able to do.
While Myiscus watched stars, Hymenaios
Watched his best friend, remembering the scene
The two had reenacted earlier.

Before other guests began to arrive,   45
Twin garlands of roses had been unbound –
Red for Hymenaios to praise Kathros,
And yellow for Myiscus to honor
A certain poet enshrined in his heart.
In a repeat of the first ritual   50
On the day he initially saw her,
The young men blessed their roses with a kiss
And bent down before Hymen's household shrine.
Its bright red Corinthian columns glowed
In the welcoming afternoon sunlight.   55
The pair of paneled doors opened once more
To the wafting tribute of burning myrrh
And bathed the bare-breasted statue within
With the pale virtue of her ivory skin
And the veneration worthy of Love.   60
Then the boys strung their respective garlands

Around the opposing columns to join
Together at the temple's pediment,
The welkin skies and flying doves painted
Within the shrine's interior once more   65
Surrounded Aphrodite's nakedness.
To clothe her in earthy glory as she
Rose from the bath of her birth – the great sea.
In repetition, each boy then knelt down
To clasp hands and silently pray to her,   70
But this time, instead of Her assistance,
The lads thanked Her for the delivery
Of their heart's desire into their arms.

"Why do you stare at me that way, Hymen?"
Snapped from his reverie, the brightest son   75
Of his holy father Helios, grinned.
"Oh, nothing, Myiscus. A wandering thought
And remembering the tribute today
Before our household shrine to Goddess Love."
"Yes, I can scent the sweet-hued blossoms now."   80
"What's wrong, Myiscus—" Hymen nearly laughed.
His friend's tone told him something troubled his mind.
"Nothing's wrong. I'm just happy for you…."
As Myiscus' volume trailed to naught,
The bright boy about to be married said   85
"I never told you how the adventure
Of me being a Little Bear ended."
"No, Hymenaios, I don't think you did."
The bright boy then let peal silvery laughter.
"You should have seen the sight when my Kathros   90
And her stern father trundled me back home.
Still pent in my feminine wig and garb.
My intended's household was all a-gasp,"
The merry tone in his friend's laughing voice
Made Myiscus turn his head and watch him: 95
"What happened when her mother first saw you?"
"Kathros' nursemaid ran over to support
The woman she was sure would faint away,
And then Stratos – the girl's father – announced

He'd given their daughter's hand in marriage   *100*
To the likes of me. But before Mother
Had a chance to chastise any of us,
I suddenly remembered they thought me
A girl, so then revealed to them slowly
My true gender; status in life; parents –   *105*
All information of which amazed them,
Especially the nursemaid, who then cried.
Kathros calmed her down, but the older one
Had suddenly come to accept the fact
That a daughter she was about to lose   *110*
To the holy ties of matrimony."
Hymen's plan had worked well, for now his friend
Smiled and laughed in his best unguarded way.
Myiscus said, "I wish I had been there."
"Me too, my friend, but"—Hymen's tone now slipped   *115*
Into the shiningly bare and sincere—
"Tomorrow, Myiscus, I want you to
Stand there by my side as I pledge my vows.
Will you do that for me, dear companion?"
"I would be honored," Myiscus confirmed.   *120*
There followed a silence with the two boys
Looking comfortably in each other's eyes,
The fountain gurgling softly to the stars.
Hymen understood his friend very well
And recognized the glint he saw in him   *125*
Which defies explanation other than
The one, greatest reason of them all – love.
He thus told Myiscus very softly:
"You are looking rather solemn tonight."
Blinking and catching a lump in this throat,   *130*
Myiscus asked his buddy plainly,
"Is it all right if I tell you something?"
"'Course it is; I'll listen to you, always."
"I'd been deceiving others and myself
To deny how I felt within my soul.   *135*
But the truth is, I love Meleager,
And that more than I love my own life, which

He pledges he loves in return for me."
No great 'told you so' moment, Hymen
Reached and took his companion's fingers. *140*
"I'm so happy for you – for both of you!"
"But I feel so foolish to have wasted – "
"Tsk, tsk, my friend. What's important is now
You have received love, and love in return
Will reward both of you with honor." *145*
"Thank you, Hymenaios." He squeezed his hand.
"Don't mention it, Myiscus, but I'm glad
You have taken the right and healthy course."
"What is it you exactly mean, Hymen?"
"I mean that the denial of the self *150*
Is a sore element of destruction
Upon a person's true self-potential.
Blinkered then by such a mindset, if we
Toss off heaven-made matches, foolishly,
We destroy everything we're meant to be *155*
For mutable customs and laws of Man.
Such limitations *must* evolve – or if
They do not, cease to bind thinking minds or
Compassionate hearts seeking to live whole."
Now letting a grin twist into a smile, *160*
Myiscus told him, "I knew you'd get it,
And that I'd been one of those, foolishly,
Hind'ring myself from what really matters."
Hymen let out a good-natured chuckle.
"I did *get* it and was waiting for you *165*
To be willing to accept it too, but –
You have, and I couldn't be happier –
And besides, just look at Meleager!
Anyone – male, female, or both – would melt
In the warm strength of such a man's heartbeat. *170*
You've made yourself and me proud by showing
You accept his love by returning it."
"Speaking of that"—Myiscus flushed bright pink—
"The gods love all love but mostly sanctify
Those willing to testify commitment, *175*
Regardless of conventions, equally.

That the union of loves, of minds, of hearts
Into one destiny is as old as the stars,
And millennia from now, it will be
Exactly the same as it is for us."   *180*
"What is it you are saying, Myiscus?"
Both young men rose to sitting positions.
"Meleager and I have discussed it,
And know in our hearts of hearts we're ready,
So if Kathros and you will grant it us,   *185*
I want *you* to be with me tomorrow
When my poet and I get married too."
Hymen's hand, open-palmed, went to his cheek,
Feeling moist heat from his friend's happy tears
Slowly sinking into his whole being.   *190*
"As proudly then," confirmed Hymenaios,
"As you stand next to my side tomorrow,
I'll be by yours, and in fact any groom

> *Whose heart of hearts most truly loves, there I'll descend*
> *And be by one and all who beckons me attend."*   *195*

PART TEN:
A DOUBLE WEDDING

Twilight of the nuptial day slowly
Was coming to its rich inheritance:
From eastern sky crept the edges of night,
While the boldness of the west continued
To send the brilliant orange and yellow rays   5
Of a proud celestial father on his
Son's most glorious of wedding parties.
On the heavenly heights of Olympus,
Hymenaios had a rise in status
As Zeus, Hera and Aphrodite draped   10
The offspring of their sun-chariot kin
With the admiring pleasure of watching
His adventures serving for the gods
Eros and Artemis with pluck and love.
The congress of immortals had gathered   15
Round the visionary well of Lord Zeus
And cheered on the defeat of human greed
By the force of mortal devotion, and
The Olympians a body then
Granted the bright demi-god and his bride   20
Deathless form to join them when Death would call.
So it was with immeasurable pride
Helios pulled his chariot across
The high arc above the Acropolis

Where families would congregate to witness 25
Beautiful children unite in wedlock.
Earlier, while He could still watch, one group
Decorated the altars of Eros
With the sweetest boughs of myrtle strong, where
Every manly blossom a poet could 30
Dedicate to the synchronized beauty
Of boys and the bold wisdoms which bless
Love-matches between the masculine tribes.
Meleager's keepsake for Myiscus
Interwove pale roses with narcissus, 35
Young vines of grape blooms, sweet-scented iris,
Fragrant marjoram amid maiden-hued
Crocus and sorrow-tainted hyacinth.
Among these bright blossoms of hope were set
Dark-leaved sprigs of laurel, ivy clusters, 40
Boughs of walnut, and sprinklings of wild thyme;
And because love among men is sometimes
Presented with a rougher road to haul,
An occasional dark-eyed violet
Rounded out the love garland to remind
A tear or two is oft shed in pursuit 45
Of a lovely lad whose heart is too hard.
In stirring fruitful contrast, the nursemaid
And doting mother of Kathros had plait
Some dear maternal drops of sentiment
Into the swag they wove as offering 50
To the earthy and fecund side of love.
For Terrestrial Aphrodite's shrine
Upon the heights of the temple complex,
They strung a garland of terebinth boughs
With globes of purple, tight-leaved artichoke, 55
Aromatic sprays of demantoid pine
With slick stalks of razor-edged-but-sweet rush.
Upon this foundation, pink-scented sprigs
Of infant apples upon their branches,
First fruit of sandstone-hued pomegranate 60
And spear-like, tapering twigs of wild pear

Were set on cushioning dollies of wheat
Golden and ripe, promising nutrition.
Interspersed with these were the proud blossoms
Of redolent cooking from the chefs: 65
Herbs dry and rich from the fields of parsley,
Sacred lovage with its scent of celery,
And the undoubtedly bawdy hing[5]
From its yellow sprays of spicy spikenard.[6]
The length of this great and fruitful garland   70
They hung around the altar of She who
Watches over earthly reproduction;
The nursemaid and Kathros' mother also
Shedding a few more tears as they did so.
But now the Sun God from his western place   75
Could begin to see the wedding procession.
It slowly went its way up the white steps
To the summit of the Acropolis –
The smoked, red-veined altar 'fore the temple
Of high-handed but loving Artemis.   80
In symbol of his absent, godly father,
Hymenaios bore three-foot tapers,
Both lit, and meant to reflect the Sun's light
On the Earth, even after darkness falls.
In token too, one torch represented   85
His deeply abiding love of Kathros
And the other as its equal among
The love of Meleager and Myiscus,
For equal, all equitable love is.
Behind the saffron-tunic'd torchbearer,   90
The wedding party slowly followed.
Up, ever up to the Goddess' steps,
They trod their way as stars came out above.

---

[5] Hing: asafoetida *(Ferula assa-foetida)*. A savory staple of Greek and Roman cuisine, in Latin is it known as *laser;* in Greek, *silphium.* Today it is best utilized in Indian cooking, thus the "hing" appellation here.

[6] Both of these tribute garlands – one to same-sex love; one to opposite-sex love – are based on *Greek Anthology* 4.1. This is the dedication of the real-life Meleager for his *Garland,* the verse collection upon which the *Greek Anthology* is based. In his tribute, he associated each plant with a poet represented in his collection of their work.

Myiscus was arrayed just like his friend,
Only his arms were laden with four wreaths,   *95*
Each bandied with verdant needles of pine –
To show the power of eternal love –
And rosebuds of yellow to signify
The budding pleasure of all earthly life.
Then behind the young men out in the lead   *100*
Came Meleager and Kathros – both in white,
While over the head of the lovely bride,
A diaphanous veil of flame colors
Was embroidered round-a-bout with living
Sprays of blooming lilies of the valley.   *105*
Next to come after the four espoused,
As many sets of parents beamed with pride.
At last mounted the white temple steps
To stand before the holy altar of
Artemis with its fragrant incense fire;   *110*
Much of the city had already come
And stood in awe to witness the nuptials.
Hymen placed his now brightly glowing lights
In slots besides the waiting high priestess.
A hush fell upon everyone, even   *115*
The tenant birds of the Acropolis.
At the signal, Hymen lifted her veil
And crowned Kathros with one of the pure wreaths.
Myiscus did the same with his beaming
Meleager, poet he'd love for life.   *120*
Once complied, their partners mirrored actions
And placed gentle crowns on their belovèds.
Both couples then joined hands for the priestess,
Who soon bound a flower garland around
The two sets of sacredly linked fingers.   *125*
"Do you," asked the pleased officiator,
"Hymen and Kathros; Meleager and
Myiscus here vow to defend in love
The person with whom you will share your life?"
"I do," rang out in affirming quartet.   *130*
"Do you also," continued the priestess,
"Avow to live in honor as equals,

Never stating your match better than that
Of your brother's? Knowing sacred is love
Arranged for each of us in heaven."   *135*
"I will," was the tender, life-sustaining
Pledge for all present – and all of mankind –
To hear now, and for every age to come.
"Then," said the priestess, "Kiss to troth your faith."
Myiscus and Meleager did so,   *140*
Starting their married life as lovingly
As each boy had pursued their long courtship.
Smiling, Hymen slapping his best friend's back,
The bright young man then raised his hand to touch
The divinely rosy cheek of Kathros,   *145*
Drawing them by slow degrees together.
They kissed, and what heart that day didn't melt?
The poet and his spouse rejoined hands, and
Myiscus, so taken with life's great joy,
Began to mutter a loud tribute: *150*
"Hymen – dear, Hymen. Come, O Hymena,"
But yet, what started as a single phrase
Others in the crowd took up as refrain;
Soon the cheer rose to fill the sky with light
And the grinning boy once more touched his wife   *155*
By her sweet flower-laced hand to draw her
Into another, longer-lasting kiss.

For then the folks did shout, rejoice and learn to say:
"Hymen, come. Hymenaios, O Hymenae!"

~

Postlude

Epithalamion

Sonnet:

But how to bring this to an open end,
To tame my emotions and reason's fight
With all the desire I must defend,
Yet be here holding you, my love, in sight.
Awake and begin our vernal weaving,
For I can barely hold you anymore
Without needing kisses for the thieving –
Awake, for what a day we have in store.
Break the tranquil cycle, come to the point
Where waits primordiality seminal
To bear down and on each of us anoint
A love more natural than chemical.
    For if ever heart loved heart and endures,
    Marry me and it will always be yours.

Poem No. 20
A Postcard for Sunny

Sonnet:

When I come to write how much I love you,
What words implore, actions must be struck,
But over the miles, I still peruse
The fleeting image of my grinning Puck.
I love you, Sunny. Let the world hear it
And never have to guess about its source;
I'll say it till every age believes it,
Shaking incredulous heads at its force.
Let vicious fate and dispatient man try
To work between the concrete bond we've mixed;
But let those who know and understand, sigh
To think the past had their love so well fixed.
    Know no space can division condescend;
    No act of God nor man can our love upend.

Poem No. 21

When those cold days come,
    the ones yet to be,
I'll keep myself warm in the place
    you've touched most sincerely.

Poem No. 22
  To Sunny
     after the departure of Selina Goh

Cursed or blessed
What things I count or don't
If they ask
I'd tell them I'd die.
I'll not deny
Never ever again
How much I love you.
If they asked
I'd say I've lived enough
If not for a single anointment.
Thinking how much you love me
I know I've lived long enough.

Poem No. 23
A Present Note

Open up my love,
and unlike a Russian box you'll see
it needs a bigger
space to fit it in comfortably.

Not like the descending requirements,
of a cube tucked down into another,
what works in me needs more than the requirements
of good ideas pruned by restless others.

Unwrap my love,
and with your own eyes look and see
it's grown the bigger
and won't fit more comfortably.

Poem No. 24

Prelude:

All through dinner, your arms were around me
While bright, funny people by example
Invited me join, but could not see
Age was not the gap, though clues were ample.
I'm not one of today's be-grungèd youth
With sloppy attire and thin gold earrings
Who wear their passions pinned in fashion proof
That they and their day have different stirrings.
The restaurant was busy; they wondered why
I seemed to grudge them company at all
Weakly trouncing the world's ways while I'd sigh
To feel your strength over me come and fall.
    For I only know I love you; that in act
    Our love long past fashion will ever live in fact.

Poem:

Desiring more than passion,
Wanting you will never be routine;
Foe of contraction,
It will bring honesty to what I mean.

How unlike shallow-but-intense
Displays of slipped reason,

Unwilling to drop their pretense,
Though youth had long changed its season,

The way the high tribute goes
Myopic vision predicts
That what hangs on knows,
It's best by the grace of what picks.

So those transitory ways
Have blundered mode onto mode
Giving silly days
Some ludicrous ways to be bold.

Habitual though they e'er,
They don't know their counterparts,
Littered here and there,
Chronicled in the human heart.

But I'll keep track above
With means stocked from within,
Knowing the truth is love
Others twist, just where it begins.

Postlude:

The world keeps making the same old mistake;
For in a quiet thought of reflection,
I see through your fingers the paths they'll take,
Never knowing they fear from projection.
But hold me close, away from the darkness,
And the errors of the day are broken
By the sweet force your thoughts can now me kiss
In a transcript no mimic thinks spoken.
So when "Do you love me?" falls from my lips,
The minute out I want to retract it
Least a faint dilemma between us slips
Via the course of a hasty habit.
  But if here I can feel you love me, then don't say,
  For I don't want to be loved any other way.

Poem No. 25

Sonnet:

Less than art, I vow to raise its better
Out of the fodder that I've said before,
But every try sits with me no better,
Ruminating the same cud as before.
I need to love you better than this,
Show not what I am, but my potential;
Reveal how much of you yearnings insist
I reach beyond death's bass role essential.
So, less than art, I fear ability
That could make a passed loved long inspire
Courage built from human fragility
That makes the dull ground repeat my desire.
    But try as I might, there won't be enough
    Matter in art to match your love enough.

Poem No. 26

Obon

Prelude

Sonnet:

All too short this sunless summer grows now
That its end taunts with a chiller view
Of the many ways my love failed, and how
I sputter sparks where a blaze is due.
For when I think how well has been your love,
And your never ceasing benevolence,
What dark shame overcomes me like a glove
Decrying guilt no inner evidence.
But how to gain the liberty I seek,
Away from just good intentions, and then –
Be bright? Though my flesh is only too weak,
You action my soul, and through it my pen.
    So then like the sputtering punk inspires,
    I'll flower uprising skies with fires.

Poem:

The body always wants,
But what it can't remember.
Just that it wants it knows,
In nothing other satisfied.

I thought I saw the dancers dance
The summer welcome for those gone,
But slowly their hands came to rest,
Their faces shining back the night's fire.

They didn't wonder why
The deed come back to light,
They only knew they knew
Heart will return to heart.

But I trapped in sunless
Wander over the same things;
One never happy, one never due
Anywhere or by anyone.

Again I say I'm sorry,
Again I say I love,
But if you can forgive,
In me my fate is doomed.

Postlude

Sonnet:

How must thought retain the time it needs
To force merit into fruition? –
Unfettered by hate and petty deeds,
Release worth from half-thought cognition?
From my bed I watch the season's pallor
Outside my window like a globe of gray,
And curse my intellect's lack of valor
Lying plagued with little hope to inveigh.
For colder times may yet come to defeat
The higher purpose that seeks renown,
But which, like autumns make summers retreat,
May grant me a time I won't let you down.
    Come my love, caress a soul into me;
    Complete what parts have most longed to be free.

Poem No. 27

Sonnet:

I'm unsure just what it is I'm doing,
Rushing in full force to greet disaster,
Shunning away from my action's pursuing
To catch catastrophe all the faster.
Sunny, I call for only you to come,
Aid me in the exorcism of youth,
Tell me what my deeds imply, what's begun
Will lose for me my only piece of truth.
But no longer do I want to suppose
The falling blows are better now than later,
Up around deceit away it all goes,
So I can be what your faith knows greater.
    Honesty, calm and settled in your plan,
    Grab me still as only love's granted can.

Poem No. 28

Tanka:

The morning rush out,
The day's readiness put on;
With we at the door
I watch him balm his lips first,
Foretasting that sweet orange kiss!

Poem No. 29

How like a time when all was fresh,
When the air turned secrets tumbling
In the breeze of promise that
"I will never die" whispered!

How like these things were the time
Between my youth and manhood
When I let the wrong go past
Before coming to the darker edge.

How like the kind of sleep I'm in,
Where none stays inspired in me,
Wandering where it thinks is good,
Resting in whom it can find.

All of these are true, and what's more,
I know it's not your forgiveness
I have the right to ask of you;
Given it, you already have.

The absolution well beyond
The wanting of it ruins me now,
And knowing if I simply ask,
You'll comfort me in your arms.

But it's I who have to forgive,
With never-failing memory
Of the smelly way I have gone,
All the time saying I loved you.

Poem No. 30

Every happy moment spent with you will
Be double-paid in sorrows to be.
Every gentle brush of your hand shall spill
A tear you'll marvel over when you see.

Poem No. 31

Tanka:

In a moment's thought,
Standing at the closet door,
That great love of his
Stretches me out as I slip
His shirt and fragrance on me.

Poem No. 32

今の愛,
今の愛 の見込み,
今のところは
それだけあげられる。

Only this love –
Only the prospects of this love –
And of this time
Is what I can offer to you.

Poem No. 33

Tanka:

Now, this time of year,
The sun at four o'clock falls
On the black slate frame
Where your arms are around me;
Warming itself on our love.

Poem No. 34

Sonnet:

Why tease we who the other loves the more,
When comparison only draws me nearer –
Around your heart – clearing off the score,
And bringing me to your soul still dearer.
Hold my hand, and let me show you something.
Bring it to the light, and there will we see,
They look so much alike – like they could sing
Of the other they hold – of the you and me.
Even if seen out in the public's mind,
When they, the ones who'd never know, deduce
Two equals holding on, they're still unkind
To love where comparison is no use.
    That in, we see so much in the other;
    Out, I'll never hide more in sham's cover.

Poem No. 35

Lyrics:

To come to this again, with words unbelieved;
which find no solace in your thought, but in
this ink that imbues me with lines believed,
to be the solitary shadow of your love again.

To come to this again; words unbelieved,
finding no solace in your thought, but in
the way the ink flows there softly pretends
the shadows of your love in me again.
What does it know that I do not? What words,
what knowing can one thought of you summon,
if not to be, if not love in words,
what the whole of love in me determines.

Know then apart we still can muster
the very thought of life in the other.

So there, and here follow the flow of you,
like the shallow depths I can only swim
so that I can recall the departed you,
and you do the same of me where distance seems to win.

Poem No. 36

Sonnet:

When the lonely hours of the night come
To afflict the poverty of your loss,
I lie awake, empty headed and dumb,
To suffer, destitute, what fate can toss.
But near your heart I long to lie my head,
To feel beneath me the pulse that gives out
A life to more than sleepy limbs in bed,
But also soul to this, and soothing to doubt.
So, isolated I wait the time now,
Counting the hard grievances of you gone;
Still, in and in, I have love anyhow
To pine under me to the light of dawn.
    And when you beat in me again, I'll know
    Deep within, my wealth of gain shall yet grow!

Poem No. 37

Sonnet:

How can my sight look but not sometimes see
How your touch loves me, but me not alone –
Why when you hold, do I forget to be
The sad boy that comfort can bemoan.
For those who have ever pondered on me,
And the numberless digits I show them,
They'll never find an answer where they see
My nervous face dart and writhe around 'em.
So when you tell me what you see of me
Is handsome, I don't care to have it said –
For a face is brief, but living beauty
Is incarnate though all that praise be dead.
    Head on your arm, for me that is the all –
    Here, our touch, our love; all questions enthrall.

Poem No. 38

Tanka:

In a crowded train;
Thirty minutes yet from you,
And none of them see –
Through their empty-hearted ways –
Just the way you will be kissed.

Poem No. 39

Sonnet:

That I will always be a fool to time –
Though in hours, days or needs it's unkind –
I know a greater drudge were I to rhyme
A word to what loves only when love's not blind.
So, I'll never be fool enough to hide
My love for you in feminine pronoun,
Or this union taken, or leave you denied,
To write a lie that belies all renown.
I love you Sunny. Let no man smother
A vow they see from one to another
When a sage preached to us as his brother,
'What merit have you, lest you love each other?'
 For no fools are we; not to time, nor want,
 But open-eyed equals to time's affront.

Poem No. 40

Sonnet:

If I take up pen again and write,
After all these soulless attempts have failed,
What merit can I expect to invite
Except that my love by ink is assailed.
We know that love and hope should equals be,
And your supply of brightness is stronger –
Deficient in the latter you see me,
But that's because I'm strong in the former.
But step-by-step, and word-by-word I try,
To cause belief in me to rise to you,
And long the day to come that when I try,
I'll master hope enough that time will love you too.
    I can speak and watch my words fall to shade,
    But the ink my love stains will never fade.

Poem No. 41

Sonnet:

Some hope for movement in the rates they watch,
Eyeing steadily the broken line rise,
While others fear their money won't be a match
For what their greedy hearts can realize.
But none of them know just how rich I am.
None of those spies of supply and demand,
Know that shallow hope a great love can fan
Or how a kindled flame can a blast withstand.
Let them grub for pennies. I have what I need.
One look around: you are there –
He who lives without love is a fool indeed,
If to try is to gain their true fair share.
    The only line I need to watch is here,
    If your eyes smile on me, all is fair.

Poem No. 42

Tanka:

Stands the old tree still –
Like people we used to know –
Thus Takasago's
Pine and the so long ago
Become friends who seem no more.

Note:

One of the major dramas of *Noh*, Zeami's play *Takasago* deals with a pair of deities, who in disguise, visit the physical incarnation of one of them, a pine tree in Takasago. There they find an old man tenderly maintaining the tree and learn how much it means to him. The story follows that this tree was separated from his lover, and that his partner pine tree was planted far away. Eventually, the gods reveal their true identities and openly rejoice that mankind can still glory in the true heart of 'poetry,' that is, in the true nature that the beauty of the universe is its central generative concept – love. From April to September 1995, Sunny and I were separated by an ocean, and thus my feelings.

Poem No. 43

Sonnet:

What misery supplies is often met
Not by cure, and much less by solution,
But it's by injury our pains get wet –
With tearful demand, comes absolution.
Like a stroll on the beach I see them come;
One care pushing the incoming beneath,
By the weak undertow, the strong grow numb,
And bathe the tides in shallow points of grief.
Yet the heart returns to a hunger bold,
And old woes sometimes new wail decries
Not letting new grief luxury in old
The way hope often better-sense denies.
  But what sorrow from us will sometimes take,
  Nothing but it can a complete love make.

Note:

Though it turned into a very un-scenic poem, the image of the tides washing in over the tops of retreating ones inspired this Sonnet. The notion itself was inspired by Shakespeare's *W. H. Sonnets* No. 60: "Like as the waves make towards the pebbled shore . . . . Each changing place with that which goes before." The date given to this poem, August 9th, 1995, is that of the main body of the sketch. I have completed it with a loose 'Sunny' quatrain (the 3rd) written at the end of 1993. The following poem, No. 44 below, was part of the original Sonnet sketch from 1993.

Poem No. 44

Two parts seem to be at fight within me,
Hope/no-hope: love and spiteful apathy.

Meaningless seems all the effort I see
Wasted in pursuits that bring in no gain;
While pretense makes the work futility
And above it all, I thump my tired brain . . .

Beach –
Water: tides erase the small imprint I've made.
One wave pushing under the might of the next,
Weakens the strong by the counter-power of the weak.

Supply and demand –
The need always seeks the cure, and of one,
A solution often injures far more than it shores up.

Poem No. 45

Prelude

I hope to bless the Fate that once blessed us
With a word deemed proper fitting's tell,
To look straight in the eyes that first saw us,
And like to the Fortunes say, you matched well.
It seems my life's on hold while I wait now,
While the hands walk around the slow hours,
Lengthening days to months, not showing how
Distillation ennobles heart-cowards.
I like them must pass around a shared eye
And see others' love under suffering,
For like them provide a voice with which to sigh
Other, better lives than just controlling.
    But my turn will come, and we will be heard;
    What They gave will one day be blessed with our word.

Poem:

Sakura

Why so long a silence
from both our pair of lips
why so hot a loneliness
when neither a word has writ.

Poem No. 46

Do I sleep or wake when I reach out –
When my arm goes out to your leg,
Or goes to bring me against
Your sleeping form, and into
Your arms that so often open
To let the wayfaring me in;
Do I wake or do I sleep when I do these –
Knowing you are not there,
But, knowing also,
Soon, you will be again.

Poem No. 47

Why so long a quiet?
As if others will be led
Into believing I care not at all;
Believe that silence bespeaks
More than all the terms
Promised, and yet,
Promised for the times
We won't have power to see.

Poem No. 48

"Here," she said to me,
A tiny glint of a smile
Peeping forth from her
All so proper composure.
"Take this and know.
Take this and I assure –
You will know
What the words of all
Those long-gone Bards
Strove to bring to life
In the death of paper, and,
The resurrection of the eyes that read."
"Take," she said, "and love
Will finally be made
More than a word
You've read once or twice."
A tiny smile glinted,
As her composure melted,
Into a little sigh,
And a little show,
Of love.

Poem No. 49
Two Fragments of an Idea

I'm not the same as I was when we met,
and maybe now I'm able to repay
the red and black flow of investments' net
that for your patience was met.

I'm not the same as I was when we met,
but proof is not put into word likely
to move a man who knows what he can get
from the investment of patience given not slightly.

Poem No. 50

Tanka:

In a simple room,
With me just looking at him,
The rest's a whirlwind –
He at center in himself,
I, all awhirl without him.

Poem No. 51

The view written from within,
    the slow seeing, the painful searching
    for the world without you.

Poem No. 52

I'm wearing his shirt,
And though the day goes badly
– Tough little I feel –
The greatness of him in me
Comes like love's breath with his scent.

Poem No. 53

Sonnet:

Why to this return after so long has passed,
And how do days to longer time extend
When we two seem to stand against the cast –
Two stones like one in a mighty current's bend.
I find the word love again trailing in ink
Behind the sweet thought of you in its tag,
The melancholy of how I fail to think
Worthy actions ever behind yours lag.
Then to this I turn again for some relief,
For shame never can stay a restless quill
When perfect charms still goad constant belief
That my love, yours its equal never will.
    Though lovers' rise can fall in quick season,
    Safe seems your love from slow time's dull treason.

www.ingramcontent.com/pod-product-compliance
Lightning Source LLC
Chambersburg PA
CBHW020937180626
46814CB00013B/1381